DRIVING MISS KENNEDY

A SAPPHIC AGE GAP ROMANCE IN THE 1940S

AVEN BLAIR

Copyright Page

CHAPTER ONE: KATE

Driving Miss Kennedy
October 1945 Savannah Georgia

S itting at my desk in the small library of my home, I hear the internal voice of my oppressor—the ugly voice I named "the black dog" years ago. I gaze at my latest published book, "Thrive: Embracing Confidence," resting on my tiger-wood desk—the beautiful desk I bought fifteen years ago when my first book was published.

The 'black dog' begins to whisper: "No one is going to buy your silly book, you fraud. You're still the same sad and depressed little girl you were years ago."

The black dog has plagued me sporadically throughout my life. I take a deep breath, close my eyes, and visualize myself at book signings. I see people telling me how much my books, speeches, and articles have helped them. Finally, he flees. He's been my nemesis since childhood, but now that I am older, I've learned how to deal with the bastard.

I quickly buzz the phone of my personal assistant, Hazel, whose office is situated on the opposite side of my home on Bull Street, in Savannah's Historic District.

She answers, "Yes, Kate?"

"Hazel, do you have my itinerary ready for the two week promotional tour?"

"Yes, ma'am, I'm finishing it now, I'll bring it to you."

"Thank you."

As I wait on Hazel I turn and look out the window that faces Bull Street and watch the gold and red leaves fall gently from the trees that line the street. It's mid October, one of my favorite times of the year.

"Here you are, Kate. This is going to be quite an undertaking visiting ten cities with more than thirty appearances either at book signings or Radio interviews."

"Yes, I agree Hazel, but I need to sell books; we have to eat, my dear."

"Oh, Kate, you could retire now at the young age of forty-four with the earnings from your self-help book sales and the speaking fees you've raked in over the past fifteen years. You're a wealthy woman, so I know you do this for the thrill and to help people. It's your gift, sweetie."

"Thank you, Hazel, but you know one of the main reasons I won't quit?"

"Is that fool haunting you again?"

"Yes, just a few moments ago," I say as I laugh.

"Kate, look behind you on your bookshelf. You've published thirteen books over the last few years. You're a huge success, a household name, Kate Kennedy, and you should know that. You tell that nemesis to go back to Hades where he belongs!"

"I smile at her and then scream out in a funny, frantic tone, 'Phantom Nemesis, Hazel St. John says, go to hell!'"

Hazel laughs and says, "Well, I didn't exactly use those words, Kate."

I hit the desk with the palms of my hands and laugh loudly. "Hazel, you're the only woman I know who is incapable of cursing at a dark entity—you're much too polite."

"Oh hush, Kate. Here's your itinerary."

I keep laughing as I glance over my jam-packed itinerary while Hazel is still standing at my side. Suddenly, I hear the deep throaty rumble of a motorcycle that reverberates through the air and eventually parks in front of my house.

"I wonder who that is?" I ask as I peer out the window and gaze at the striking beauty dismounting her motorcycle. My heart begins to race. I'm completely captivated as I watch this young, beautiful woman in tight khaki pants, hugging her curves divinely and tucked perfectly inside a pair of Jodhpur boots. She pushes her fingers through her hair, shakes those dark, loose curls, and then swaggers all the way up my driveway, and into my gut.

"That must be Vita," Hazel says as she shakes her head.

"Vita?!…Our Vita?" I breathlessly ask in a shout as I watch Hazel leave the room. Then I glance back at that beast she rode in on.

I bark at Hazel, "You better bring her over here."

I hear a faint, "I will," as Hazel makes her way back across the house to let Vita in through the side door of her office.

My gosh the last time I saw Vita she was about eighteen. The gorgeous woman who strutted up my driveway can't possibly be Hazel's granddaughter, little Vita.

I hear them talking inaudibly for a few minutes as I wait to get a better look at what just peeled up Bull Street and sucker punched me. Their voices are getting closer so I stand and take a deep breath.

"Hazel, you cannot tell me this is little Vita."

"Hi Miss Kennedy," she says.

"You better come over here and give me a hug, Vita." She smiles sweetly at me, walking gracefully toward my open arms, politely leaving the swagger outside. Hell, I didn't mind, I loved watching her strut all the way up my sidewalk.

Vita meets my eyes with sweet intensity before she wraps those enticing arms around me. She gives me a strong hug. I do not recognize this woman as the Vita I knew years ago. The woman in my arms is a beautiful and grown young woman who is making my heart pound as I pull her close to me.

As I pull back I look at her, fully. "Vita, my gosh, honey, you are absolutely gorgeous! The last time I saw you I believe you were marching for women's rights. What are you rebelling against these days?" I ask in a playful tone.

She laughs and then quickly says, "Anything I don't agree with, Miss. Kennedy."

We all three laugh.

Hazel shakes her head and interjects, "You would think a young lady in a graduate theology program wouldn't be so rebellious, dress like this, or ride a dang motorcycle."

"I love your motorcycle, Vita. Come outside and show it to me."

"Well sure, Miss Kennedy."

"Okay, stop right there, Vita. You're a grown woman now so you must call me Kate."

She gazes at me, and I quickly see a playful charm emerge into a grin. The phone rings and Hazel retreats back to her office to answer it leaving us alone.

"Well, OK, I will definitely call you Kate." She grabs my hand and says, "Come on, I'll show you my Indian."

"Your Indian!?"

Vita's laugh is delightful as she pulls me toward the front of the house. "Yes, it's a brand of motorcycle. It's an Indian Scout, and I love it."

We make our way to the sidewalk, and I notice that Vita has regained some of the swagger she left behind earlier. I like it. Her confident walk in those boots, and those sexy dark curls atop a motorcycle, aren't something you see in a woman every day.

"Well, here she is, Kate.".

"Wow, Vita, this bike is amazing, and it definitely suits you. I love the British green color and the leather seat looks very comfortable."

"It is! I rode it from Atlanta a few days ago. I am taking the semester off. I need a break, plus I butted heads with one of my professors last semester so I thought I would vanish for a bit. I'm staying with Grandma through Christmas."

"Hmmm, butted heads, huh?" I ask as I grin at her.

Vita laughs as she shakes her head allowing those lovely curls to dance. She glances back at my house then whispers, "Shhh, Grandma doesn't know any of this, she would skin me alive."

"Well, Vita, there is nothing wrong with challenging authority occasionally. If you feel that your ideas are valid and morally right, then you should never let anyone sway you otherwise."

She looks at me seriously with those brooding dark eyes as she sits comfortably on her motorcycle. "Thank you, Kate," she says softly.

It gets quiet for a moment. The silence allows our eyes to intermingle, communicating what words could never express. I fold my arms as I continue gazing into her eyes, never wanting to release them.

Then my mind shames me as I think: What in the hell am I doing? This is little Vita, Hazel's Granddaughter. So I release her sweet eyes and ask, "So, Vita, what are you going to do for the next few months?"

"Ride my bike, go to the beach, and be a total bum."

I laugh loudly at her confident charm. "Well, you are young my dear, so you are allowed to take as much time off as you need. I wish I could be more carefree."

"What's holding you back, Kate?"

"Oh hell, Vita. My life isn't my own anymore. I write constantly, speak, do book signings, and give radio interviews. I can't remember when my days and weeks were not planned out." I tell her as I search those dark eyes of hers.

She reaches for my arm, looks into my eyes again and softly says, "The greatest hazard of all, losing one's self, can occur very quietly in the world, as if it were nothing at all."

"That sounds familiar, Vita. Who said that?"

"Søren Kierkegaard," she says softly.

"Hmmm, I think I can understand why you might be butting heads with professors in the theology department if Kierkegaard is perhaps your idol."

Vita laughs loudly and says, "You nailed it! I adore his philosophy. And his challenge and critique of organized religion."

"Why theology, Vita?"

"My love for Our Creator, Kate. I want to know the true nature of God. It's as simple as that. I know that is something I can never completely achieve, but I love trying."

I shake my head at her youthful wisdom, "That's beautiful, Vita."

She smiles tenderly at me and says, "Tell Grandma that I'll meet her at seven for dinner. Hey, you want to come too? We are having dinner at Forsyth Grill."

My heart flips as I look down at the pavement for a bit knowing I should say no, but I don't. I look at her and say, "Well, I better ask Hazel."

Vita dismounts her bike and then quickly pushes down fast and firmly on the kickstart lever with her foot. I hear the same deep throaty rumble she rode in on. "Kate, Grandma would love it if you joined us, you know that. And I definitely would."

Shaking my head I smile and say, "Perhaps, I will. It sounds like fun."

"That's great! I'll see you at seven then," she says with a smile. I remain standing on the sidewalk, watching that beautiful creature ride up Bull Street, my heart filled with tender pain and complete admiration.

Sitting back at my desk, I find myself peering out the window, thinking about Vita and the wise quote she shared from Kierkegaard.

"Kate!" Hazel shouts frantically as she dashes in the room.

"Oh, gosh, Hazel! You scared the bejesus out of me!"

"I'm sorry honey, but we have a problem!" Hazel says frantically, her voice tinged with urgency.

"What's wrong, Hazel?"

"It's John, he's in the hospital with pneumonia. Carol said they have started him on antibiotics and fluids."

"Oh, that's just awful," I say.

"I know. Your tour is in three days and you don't have your driver, Kate!"

"Well, I appreciate your concern Hazel, but at the moment I am more concerned with John and Carol."

"I know. I am too. It's just that my job as your assistant is to make sure everything in your life flows smoothly. I wasn't thinking."

"Oh, Hazel. Honey, you're a gem. Did she say if she'd call back and let us know more?"

"Yes, she said she would let us know how everything goes."

"Good! Hazel, send a fruit basket to the hospital, please."

"I sure will. I'll do it now." Hazel turns to head back to her office and then stops and turns around. "Kate, we do need to find you another driver before Monday."

"Yes, I know," I say nodding. "Oh Hazel, Vita said she would meet you at the restaurant at seven and she invited me. Is that okay?"

"Hazel puts her hand on her hips and looks at me above those tiny readers of hers and says, "Kate Kennedy, are you serious? Honey, you are family!" She then shakes her head at me.

I smile and then nod my head at her. As she leaves I turn and gaze back out my window and think about John and all the fun times he and I have had on our numerous tours these past several years. I have no idea who I can find to replace him, but I know it will get sorted out before Monday. I turn off the lights in my library and head upstairs to get ready for dinner with Vita and Hazel.

CHAPTER TWO: VITA

R iding my Indian Scout into Grandma's driveway I park it and then head inside to dress for dinner with her and Kate. On my drive from Kate's home to here I took a short detour along the coast. As I smelled the saltwater and inhaled the October breeze my head was full of freedom and Kate Kennedy. Damn, what a woman!

Walking into the shower I feel the warm water flow over my body. All I can think about is that gorgeous woman and how she felt in my arms. I place my hands against the wall to steady myself as I replay our eyes dancing in tune as she stood gracefully on the sidewalk, arms crossed, gazing at me intensely. There's no way in hell that gorgeous blonde didn't feel the magic between the two of us.

It felt nice and familiar having Kate's lovely gray eyes on me again. When I was a teenager, I had an awful crush on her that developed into love by the time I was seventeen—a love that I haven't quite gotten over. Of course I never told her, but somehow I knew she felt it from me.

It's been years since I've seen her because I live in Atlanta now and only visit grandma a couple of times a year. She looked at me quite differently today than she did all those years ago, that much I know. I can't help but smile. This time while I'm here I'm going to make damn sure she knows how I feel.

As I push my foot into a black leather loafer, I button my black and white houndstooth pants not knowing what blouse to wear. Searching my closet I find a nice solid white top and my black cardigan that I adore. I throw them on the bed and go back to the bathroom to work on my makeup. Keeping it subtle I just opt for a bit of eyeshadow, mascara, and lipstick.

Looking at my lips, I think of Kate. What would appeal to this mature woman without making it obvious that I went to extreme lengths for a simple dinner? Or perhaps maybe I should let her know I dressed especially for her. My head is a muddle. I quickly decide to be brave so I apply a bit of dark lipstick emphasizing my top lip. Shaking my head, I rake my fingers through my curls as I blot my lips together.

I gaze in the mirror and smoothly ask, "Damn, who are you sexy?" Then I laugh at myself.

Turning off the engine on my motorcycle, I remove my helmet and immediately begin to run my fingers through my hair. Wearing the helmet was an attempt to keep my hair in place. Normally, I couldn't care less how my hair tangles when I ride my motorcycle, but tonight is different.

As I walk into the restaurant, I see Grandma and Kate at a secluded table in the back, talking. I approach slowly. Kate turns her head when I am halfway to their table. Her lovely eyes merge with mine again, just as they did on the sidewalk earlier. I hold her intense gaze as I feel butterflies flipping in my stomach. Taking a deep breath I reach their table. Kate stands and kisses my cheek. Wow, I didn't see that coming, but I immediately kiss her cheek as well. Then I sit in the chair next to Grandma.

"Hi Grandma," I say as I place my arms around her and kiss her cheek too.

"You look very nice tonight, Vita," Grandma says with a smile.

"Well, Thank you Grandma," I say, then look across the table at the most beautiful woman in the restaurant.

"I agree, you do indeed look very lovely tonight, Vita," Kate says with a sweet grin. I feel a bit embarrassed but I hold onto my confidence and Kate's radiant gray eyes.

"Thank you, Kate," I say as I smile at her.

"The two of you looked like you were having an intense conversation when I entered the restaurant. Is everything okay?"

"John is in the hospital, you remember, Kate's driver."

"Oh yes, what happened to him?"

"Pneumonia," Grandma says.

I look at Kate and say, "Oh gosh, what about your promotional tour?"

"That's what we are trying to figure out, honey," Grandma says.

Our waiter approaches asking for my drink order. I see that Kate and Grandma both have wine so I order a chardonnay.

"Do you have a back-up driver, Kate?"

She shakes her head as she takes a sip of her wine.

Our waiter approaches our table again and takes our meal order then leaves.

Things get quiet for a moment as we all sip on our wine. Taking a deep breath, I look straight at Kate and say, 'I'll do it.'"

Kate seems to freeze in her seat, but I hold onto her eyes,

not allowing her to think this is a bad idea. She probably is thinking that, but I continue to gaze into those gorgeous gray eyes anyway.

Grandma says, "Vita, honey, I don't think that's a good Idea."

While looking at Kate I ask, "Why not?"

Kate looks at Grandma but remains silent. So I turn and look at Grandma and say, "Grandma, I have almost three months off with nothing to do, there is no reason I can't do this."

"Well, Vita, you are more than capable of driving and navigating a car, honey. It's just that John, as a male, also serves as a bodyguard for Kate and fills in as her assistant, ensuring she meets her commitments on time."

I glance at Kate, "What's your opinion?"

She takes a sip of wine, most likely taking a minute to ponder this. "Well, I don't know Vita." Then she looks at Grandma and says, "Hazel, it would solve my problem."

I want to jump across the table and hug this awesome woman. She knows exactly how to handle Grandma. That was the perfect answer.

"Hazel, I like the idea of Vita stepping in, however, I am going to let the two of you discuss this. I see William Abernathy over at the bar. There is something I need to ask him so you and Vita talk this over while I'm gone. Okay?"

Kate gives me a soft gaze before she rises to leave. Perhaps that was the best choice for her, I know she would never interfere with Grandma's decisions if they involve her family.

I look at Grandma and ask, "Why don't you want me to do this? I don't understand."

Grandma turns her chair toward me and glances over at the bar where Kate is then she looks back at me. "I just don't think it's a good idea, honey."

"You've said that twice. I'm a twenty-eight year old graduate student with a good head on my shoulders, Grandma. Why are you against this?"

Grandma looks away for a moment and I remain silent knowing I deserve an answer. "Honey, Kate left the table to allow me to explain something to you."

I look over my shoulder and see Kate laughing as she talks with the gentleman. I glance back at Grandma. "Is this because she's a lesbian?"

"Grandma whips her head towards me quickly and sharply. 'What?! You know this?! How?!'"

Oh hell, how am I going to explain to Grandma why I know this? I can't say, 'It takes one to know one.' I just look at her and say, "Grandma, I'm a grown woman and I can put two and two together." Hopefully, she will buy this.

"I suppose that is the reason, Vita. I have an uneasiness about you driving her," she says as she looks at her wine then takes a sip.

"Grandma, Kate is a wonderful person. You can't allow this to be the reason for not wanting me to be her driver, that is completely unfair."

She doesn't say anything for a bit and I remain silent as I continue looking at her. She shakes her head and says, "You're right Vita. Kate has been nothing but good to me over the last fifteen years. And she is indeed a wonderful person, I'm ashamed that I said no. Vita you will make an excellent choice for her."

"Oh Grandma, you are such an amazing woman, thank you. It's going to be so much fun!"

"Now Vita, this isn't a vacation road-trip, honey. This is serious business and Kate is a complete professional when she's out on the road. I need you to keep her on track and be punctual at all times. She will rely on you immensely."

"Yes ma'am, I intend to do just that. Thank you for your

faith in me," I say as I hug her. I glance over at the bar and meet Kate's eyes. I give her a smile and a small nod. She smiles back at me and I think I see a bit of shyness. It only lasted a second but it melted my heart. As she approaches I turn back to Grandma and wait for her to sit.

"So what's the verdict, Miss Hazel?"

"Well, I think Vita is a perfect choice, I'll give her a copy of your itinerary and brief her over the weekend."

"Brief me? This sounds like a CIA mission."

Kate chuckles and then looks at Grandma as the two of them laugh loudly at me. It's sweet watching their chemistry together. And their love and admiration for one another.

"Let's make a toast," I say as I smile at Kate. "What's our final destination?"

"New York City," Kate says.

"Okay, then we will toast to safe travels, all the way to New York City."

"Here, Here!" Says Kate.

"Safe travels!" adds Grandma.

Our food arrives and Kate and I spend the remaining time during dinner trying to keep our gazes at a minimum. I'm sure she knows that Grandma had to tell me she's a sapphist. Thank goodness Grandma didn't inquire about my sexual preference or there would have been no way in hell she would have allowed this.

"Well, I am tired ladies so I am headed home. How about you Vita?" Grandma asks.

I stand to hug Grandma goodbye and say, "I'll be along soon, Grandma. I want to talk with Kate a bit longer about her expectations of me."

Grandma leaves, and I sit back in my chair, looking

across the table again at Kate. She takes her last sip of wine, emptying the glass as she gazes at me. I smile at her and begin to feel a bit shy amidst the silence.

"Kate, thank you for your confidence in me, I won't let you down."

Kate holds onto her empty wine glass, rocking it back and forth as she gazes at me, then says, "Oh, Vita, you could never let me down, honey. I am flattered that you want to be my driver and assistant over the next two weeks. It can get a bit grueling on the road. I am very thankful that I'm going to have someone with me whom I know and can trust. It's a big relief."

"Are you kidding, I am excited. Grandma mentioned that John is a bodyguard as well. Perhaps I won't be as skillful as John is, however, I did deck a guy about two months ago for being a wise-ass."

Kate burst out with a deep belly-laugh. "Vita, my gosh. You have indeed grown up since I last saw you, honey. And I don't even want to know the circumstances. I'm sure the guy deserved it." She continues laughing and then adds, "You have officially passed the qualifications as bodyguard."

We both laugh hysterically as we clink our empty wine glasses together.

CHAPTER THREE: KATE

D riving home from the restaurant, I begin to smile as I think about how delightful and charming Vita is. Then, I begin laughing as I visualize her decking that poor guy. Goodness, she must be more of a spitfire than I can imagine. Hopefully, she won't need to deck anyone during our trip, but I might actually get a thrill out of watching that gorgeous brunette with her dark velvety eyes punch a guy out. I continue laughing almost uncontrollably as I turn into my driveway.

Walking into my home a new self-help book title pops into my head as I continue my laughter. *Knockout Queen: A Lady's Guide to Punching Problems Away.* "Oh lord, Kate Kennedy, what have you gotten yourself into?" I ask myself out loud as I head to the kitchen for a glass of iced tea.

As I rest in my club chair in the living room my thoughts are still on Vita. My laughter subsides and I begin to think about what my real reasons are for being completely elated that I'll be sharing the next two weeks with her. Hell, I like Vita, I tell myself, which is very true. How could anyone not like Vita?

Yes, I am attracted to her, I can't lie to myself. But I know how demanding my commitments are so that will keep my mind occupied, it usually does. Hell, it always does. Writing, speaking and interviews are all I think about these days. Especially since my breakup with Helen three years ago.

As I climb the stairs to retreat for the evening, thoughts of Helen and how everything went so badly flood my mind. It's become clear to me that having a lasting love of my own seems impossible; my professional life demands too much. No good woman has been willing to compete with my drive for success, especially over these recent years. I don't blame them—I wouldn't try either.

While packing my toiletries, I hear the side door open in Hazel's office.

"We're here, Kate," Hazel shouts out. I pause to look at myself in the mirror for a moment. I scrutinize my age lines, discriminately. Damn, they seem to get deeper every passing year. Then I wonder why I'm criticizing myself this morning. I know perfectly well why—'V-I-T-A.' I grab my bags and head downstairs to greet them. Yes, I am older now, but I know that I'm still an attractive woman so I smile at myself quickly, then head down to greet them.

"Good morning, ladies," I say in an elated voice as I greet Vita and Hazel in her office.

"Good morning, Kate," Vita says, offering me a huge smile and hug.

"Hi Kate, Hazel quickly adds while looking over my itinerary.

"Kate, Grandma has grilled and briefed me all weekend. I am at your service ma'am."

I laugh and say, "Grilled you? Hazel, my heavens I'm

surprised Vita showed up this morning. What on earth did you grill her about?" I ask, shaking my head and smiling at Vita.

"Oh hush you two," she says as she shakes her head. I just wanted to make sure Vita has a realistic picture of what is expected of her and what her duties are."

While Hazel's continues glancing over the itinerary I quickly look at Vita and give her a wink and a grin. She covers her mouth to keep from laughing out loud.

Vita recovers quickly and then asks, "Where are the car keys, Kate? I'll move the Packard closer and open the trunk for our luggage."

"Oh yes, let me get those." Vita follows me toward the kitchen for the keys. As I hand them to her I say, "Hopefully Hazel didn't 'grill' you too hard all weekend."

"No, she didn't, I was teasing her. By the way, Kate, you look absolutely stunning this morning," Vita says sweetly to me, glancing at my attire and then meeting my eyes with those lovely dark, velvety eyes of hers.

"Thank you, Vita. That's very sweet of you."

She takes the keys and then quickly says, "It ain't sweet honey, it's the absolute truth." She smiles at me before turning to leave and go move the car, leaving me standing in the kitchen with a stomach full of butterflies and complete affection for this lovely young woman. I smile and shake my head as I flip off the kitchen light, knowing that the next couple of weeks with Vita are going to be quite interesting.

Vita and I are on our way to the first city on my book tour, Charleston. As I sit in the back of my Packard I can't help but gaze at Vita's loveliness and smile. I'm used to staring at the back of John's head. While John is my friend and I love him dearly, having this beautiful young woman driving me feels amazing.

"Do you enjoy these road trips, Kate?"

"Well, yes I do. They can get monotonous at times, but greeting the people who actually read my books is very rewarding."

"That's wonderful hearing you say that after all the years of doing this," Vita says.

I laugh and she quickly interjects, "Oh, hell, Kate I wasn't implying….."

"Vita, honey, I am well aware of my age and how long I have been doing this."

"Kate, you don't look a day over thirty-five, and that's the absolute truth."

I smile as I glance out the window enjoying her sincere flattery. "Well, thank you, Vita."

"I believe this is our first stop up ahead, WLCB, I'll park as close as I can," Vita says. I look at my new book on the seat beside me and smile.

Before I grab my book and prepare to open my door I glance over quickly as I hear the back door open. I look and see Vita smiling and holding the door open for me. Those butterflies must have followed me from the kitchen earlier, because they are back and it feels as though they brought some friends along.

As I exit I stand and look at Vita closely admiring her apparel. She is wearing a dark brown tailored suit jacket that is fitted with a defined waistline. I smile at her and whisper, "By the way, you look stunning today as well, Vita."

She smiles at me and softly says, "Thank you, Kate."

"You're welcome, sweetie. But, I must admit, I miss you in your khaki pants and especially those leather motorcycle boots you wore Friday."

Vita grins and winks at me sweetly, then says, "Don't worry, I packed them."

Oh hell, I just got goosebumps. "You did? Hmmm." That's all I can utter as my mind begins to contemplate on why she would pack those. I just shake my head and smile at her.

Vita grabs and opens the door to the station just as John would have done. I smile thinking Hazel must have prepped poor Vita all weekend. I'm sure she did, I know Hazel.

"Hello, Miss Kennedy, we are happy to have you back with us again," says the station manager, Robert as we enter the lobby.

"Thank you, Robert. I appreciate you allowing me to speak with your audience again. I always enjoy coming here."

I glance back and see Vita standing by the door obviously knowing she is to wait in the lobby for me. I smile at her before Robert escorts me to the 'studio.'

I've completed two radio interviews and Vita has been nothing but a complete pro and a delight. "I'm hungry, Vita. How about you?"

"Starving!" She says loudly.

I laugh at her and say, "good, what would you like to eat?"

"You pick, Kate. You know this area, I wouldn't have a clue where to go."

"Up ahead is Folly Road, take it, please."

Vita turns onto Folly Road which will take us toward Folly Beach. Remembering that Vita said she was going to visit the beach during her time off I can't resist taking her there myself.

"Oh, Kate! Here's the beach!"

I smile at her excitement, pleased that I'm making her

happy. "It is indeed. Over to your right is *The Sandcastle Restaurant*. They have excellent food, so pull in there, Vita."

Vita and I sit in a booth towards the back of the restaurant. It's well past the lunch crowd so it's just us and a few others here.

The waitress sits a huge burger and fries in front of Vita and I laugh realizing she is indeed young and doesn't have to worry about what she eats yet.

"All you're eating is that salad, Kate?"

"Well, I'll eat again later," I say as I chuckle watching her stuff that burger in her mouth.

"Good, then I'll get a chocolate shake with my next burger," Vita says as she laughs at herself.

"Oh, Vita. You're hilarious. I sure miss the days when calories didn't matter."

"Kate! Really?"

"What?"

"You're fit and lean; you could eat a burger with me if you wanted to. Do you want a bite?" Vita asks, extending her arm with the burger in hand, enticing me.

I look at her burger knowing full well she doesn't expect me to take a bite. So I grip her wrist gently and lean in and take a huge bite from her burger as I gaze into those smooth velvety eyes of hers. Vita seems to freeze as she watches my mouth on her burger and my eyes on hers.

I let go of her wrist and sit back as I chew on my huge bite of her delicious burger, grinning inside. I smile as I watch her frozen body, arm still extended and the burger right where I left it. Vita is speechless for a moment then whispers, "You just surprised the hell out of me, Kate."

I burst into laughter as I swallow that nice big bite of her burger. Vita shakes her head, bringing herself back to reality. She then holds my gaze as she takes a huge bite of her burger.

We both start laughing again as Vita tries her best not to choke on the massive bite she just inhaled.

"You're too much, Vita," I say as I continue laughing and enjoying those exquisite eyes of hers.

After we are back in the car I instruct Vita where to turn allowing us access to the beach with our car. "I love late evenings at the beach, Kate. Thank you for bringing me out here."

"You're welcome, love." Oh hell, I just called her 'love.' Why did I do that? I need to be more careful. Well after the burger encounter, what did I expect? Vita isn't acting any differently, thank goodness.

I grab my small travel pillow and stretch out on the back seat like I often do on these trips. The breeze from the ocean feels so nice with all the windows down.

"Kate, take a nap if you'd like. I have my eyes open and I'm alert."

"That's sweet Vita, I might just do that. I believe we have two hours until the book signing at *Inkwell Books*. Don't let me sleep longer than forty-five minutes though, okay?

"Sure thing, I have my watch set."

I feel completely safe with Vita, so I close my eyes and drift off.

As I sit at the table in *Inkwell Books* I greet my lovely readers and sign their copies of my latest book. I notice Vita is standing behind me over to the side. This was indeed a great idea having Vita as my driver and even my 'bodyguard.' I giggle as I think again about her decking that guy.

The last few minutes are approaching and the Bookstore owner comes to my table thanking me for stopping by. Vita and I gather our things and within a flash we are back in the Packard and headed toward Mount Pleasant.

"The motel is just ahead, Vita."

"Yes, I see it. *Shoreline Cabins*, correct?"

"Yes, pull in and I'll go inside and check us in."

"Well, I'm coming with you," Vita says insistently.

I just smile as I grab my clutch and then open my door. Vita is standing there holding my door. I step out and face her and say, "You don't have to open my door every time, Vita."

"Yes, I do. You're my responsibility, Miss Kennedy."

I suck in my cheeks and grab them with my teeth to keep from smiling too big. Why did I enjoy the way that sounded? 'You're my responsibility.'

We're greeted by a smiling lady as we enter the office of the motel.

"Hello, I'm Kate Kennedy and we have reservations for tonight. I believe we have two rooms."

"Yes, Miss Kennedy. My name is Ann and you do indeed. And we are happy to have you here, I've read many of your books."

Smiling at her I say, "I sure hope they were helpful."

"They were indeed. I wouldn't have had the courage to buy this motel without some of the things I read in your books."

"Wow, Ann. I don't know what to say. That makes me extremely happy, especially helping a woman so much. This is a charming motel, you should be extremely proud of yourself."

She smiles at me and says, "I am, thank you."

Ann gives us our keys and directs us to where our two small cabins are.

As we follow the road to our cabin Vita says, "Kate, how

your writing encouraged that woman back there makes me so proud to know you."

"Oh, love. That's very sweet of you to say." I close my eyes repeating *Vita-Vita-Vita* over and over in my head so I won't call her 'love' again.

Our cabins are sitting side-by-side, which makes me happy knowing she will be only a few yards away. I do like Vita very much and enjoy her as a woman, but on these trips having someone who is watching out for me makes me feel very safe. And I already feel safe with Vita after only one day.

Vita helps me inside my cabin with one of my suitcases and my vanity case. "You need some food, Vita?"

"Well, I suppose. How about you?"

As I look at her I notice her sweet brown eyes look so very tired. "You look tired, Vita. Are you okay?"

"Sure, I'm fine. We probably do need to get a bit of food."

"Yes, we do. Come on, there is a diner just about a mile up ahead. We'll grab a quick bite and then retire for the evening. Okay?"

Vita gives me a grin as I grab her hand and walk her to the door. When we reach the car Vita opens the back door for me to enter but I stand close to her and shut the door and grin. Then I say come on as I turn quickly and hop in the front seat.

After Vita gets in she asks, "why aren't you riding in the back?"

"We're off duty, Vita. Now we are just two friends going for a burger," I say sweetly to her. She smiles at me and I see a bit of shyness. She quickly releases my eyes and cranks the Packard then drives forward, toward the Diner.

CHAPTER FOUR: VITA

L ying in bed, my mind and body are completely exhausted after such a long day. I know Kate doesn't drive on these trips, but I wonder how she manages to do this year after year. She obviously loves it. Thinking about the lady who owns this motel and the kind words she had for Kate brings a smile to my face.

Watching her interact with her loyal readers today made me realize just how much I admire not only her, but Grandma as well. Those two are a power-team. I've always been proud of Grandma, but after seeing a glimpse of what goes into these tours I quickly realize why she was so serious with me all weekend.

I'm extremely tired so I pull the covers up, flip on my side, and then close my eyes. The afternoon at the beach with Kate was wonderful. I enjoyed watching the waves crash, and the seagulls chattering. But what I loved most was gazing at Kate through my rearview mirror as she napped. I eased the mirror downward as soon as she drifted off to keep my eyes on her.

All I could do was stare at that gorgeous woman and

wonder how those perfect lips of hers would taste. Kissing her lips is something that I've thought about for years. With that sweet thought, I sigh, then drift off in complete bliss.

As I finish with my makeup I hear a knock on my cabin door. I open the door and standing in front of me looking like a million bucks is the famous Kate Kennedy. She is grinning at me and holding two cups of coffee. Giving her a bright and cheerful smile I say, "Good Morning, Miss Kennedy."

She gives me a huge grin as she enters my cabin. "Well, good morning to you, Miss St. John," she says cheerfully. "Coffee?" she asks, offering me the cup. As I take my coffee from her, our eyes sync, silently saying good morning to one another. My heart begins to flip, waking the butterflies.

"How did you sleep?" I ask.

"Gloriously!"

"Good, we have a long day again so I am very glad you slept well."

Kate sits on my bed, crosses those long legs of hers, and gazes at me as she sips her coffee. "How about you, Vita. Did you rest well?"

"Yes I did. I didn't wake until my alarm went off, so I am well rested and ready for another day on the road with you."

She continues smiling at me. "I'm glad you slept well." She pauses for a moment and I sit beside her on the bed. She turns toward me and softly says, "I'm glad you're with me, Vita."

As I look into those lovely gray eyes I hold onto them and say, "So am I, Kate. I've admired you forever, you know."

"You have? I didn't know that, Vita."

I sip my coffee, take a deep breath, and say, "Kate, I have all of your books and have read every one of them."

"Oh, Vita. Seriously? I don't know what to say. I mean it's usually older individuals who read my books. I never thought that you would even be interested in reading one."

"I've always been interested in you, Kate," I say softly. I say no more, allowing her to discern that comment for herself.

"Hmmm, that's sweet, Vita," she says as she touches my back and gently rubs it for a few seconds. "Are you packed and ready?" She asks.

"Yes, ma'am, I am ready."

"Great! Let's drive for a short while and then eat breakfast. Is that okay?"

"Of course, I'm sure you know exactly where you want to eat breakfast. Since you've done this many times you obviously know all of the best places to eat."

"I do indeed. So let's be off."

As I drive back up the trail toward the main road Kate asks me to stop at the office for a bit. I watch her walk inside with our keys and one of her books. When she comes out she is smiling and doesn't have her book any longer. I smile knowing she must have given it to Ann, the lady who owns the motel. My heart continues to fill with admiration and complete affection for her.

After breakfast we head toward our next destination, Wilmington, North Carolina.

"Vita, we have two brief radio spots in Wilmington mid afternoon and then a two hour book signing at *Port City Bookshop*."

"Yes, I have it all mapped out for us, Kate."

"Vita, you are a marvel. Hell, I might just have to let John go and hire you full-time. You've been amazing."

"Kate, I know you would never let go of John, but hearing you say that makes me very happy."

Her eyes meet mine in the rearview mirror. I glance

intermittently between the road and her lovely eyes that have kidnapped my attention. Kate continues to smile at me, then gives a quick wink before turning her head to gaze out her window.

That felt incredible, whatever that intense moment was. Shaking my head a bit, I try to refocus on reality and my driving. I'm not sure what just happened, but I know I want more of that.

∾

"Vita, I believe we are about an hour away from Wilmington, so why don't we stop for a quick lunch."

"Okay, but I'm never going to fit into my khaki motor-cycle pants after this trip, Kate."

"Well, I'll have to start feeding you salads instead of burg-ers, because I like how those khaki's fit you, love."

My feminine core just kicked me hard; damn, this woman is unreal. Not only does she make such a sensually flattering comment but she followed it with 'love.' That's the third time she has called me that. I take a deep breath and glance in my rearview mirror. Kate gives me another smile. I exhale that deep breath as I turn into the roadside diner she mentioned.

Sitting in the diner booth with Kate I glance at the menu quickly and then order a salad when the waitress arrives.

"Vita, I was kidding about the salads."

"Well, I wasn't. I mean, sure I am a burger lover, but I'll gain ten or fifteen pounds if I continue consuming hamburgers and fries every day. Plus, I know you weren't kidding."

She looks oddly at me.

Looking straight into her eyes I say, "I know you love how those khakis fit me, you weren't kidding about that."

Kate clears her throat, sips some water, then her eyes

follow her glass as she sits it softly against the table. She then raises those sexy gray eyes to meet mine. Grins at me and whispers, "You're right, I was definitely not kidding about that, love."

This moment feels incredible as our eyes tenderly hold one another. I whisper, "I like it when you call me that."

Kate smiles at me, then nods gently acknowledging that she also likes calling me that. We sit and wait on our food in silence and complete contentment. My feelings for Kate have just intensified in an instant. How did this happen so fast?

I have admired, and admit that I have loved Kate for years. And then Friday I was completely attracted to her sensually, as a woman, but now, what is this? What's happening to us? To me?

I've been trying to keep myself in check and remain completely professional with her. We've had a couple of flirtatious moments, but I want her to know she can rely on me.

"Kate?"

"Yes, love?"

"I'm sorry?"

"For what, Vita?"

I look out the window for a bit then back at her. "For the comment about how the Khakis look on me. I want to remain professional and not let you down."

"Vita, you have been completely professional. I'm the one who originally made the comment about your khaki pants, so If anyone should apologize it ought to be me." Kate waits a moment then says, "But, I won't apologize, because I do indeed love how those pants fit your lovely body. And I'm also enjoying how I feel when I'm with you."

Smiling at her I feel a tear pooling.

"Vita, my love. It's okay. Should I have not said those things to you?"

Shaking my head, "No, it makes me happy, and I feel the same, Kate."

The waitress places our salads in front of us. We thank her and then our eyes meet again. This time I wink at her and she seems to blush a bit. We both giggle and then begin eating. That tender moment was completely magical, but I know for her benefit on this trip I'll need to keep myself in check.

"So, we are staying in Wilmington tonight, correct?" I ask.

"Yes, we are and I was going to let it be a surprise, but I'l tell you now."

"Tell me what, Kate?" I ask with excitement.

"It's a motel on the beach."

"Seriously?! No way! I love the beach at night. Well, hell I love it at any time of day."

"I know you do," she whispers to me.

Smiling at her I ask, "Will you walk the beach with me tonight?"

"Of course, silly!"

Within a few minutes my tummy is full along with my heart as I drive us to Wilmington for her next engagements. As we reach the city I smile knowing that within a few hours I will have Kate all to myself. And we will be at the beach, officially 'off duty' again.

Driving towards our motel for the evening I feel somewhat tired, but also elated that Kate's engagements for the day are over. She is officially mine for the night and I can't wait to walk the beach with her.

"It's been a long day, are you tired?" I ask.

"I will be when it's time for bed, that's for sure."

"You're amazing at book signings, Kate. The people love you so much."

"Awww, Vita, thank you. I enjoy meeting my readers. That part of my job is easy. Writing books is the harder part."

I laugh. "I understand, writing the numerous papers required in my master's program can be daunting."

"Oh, Vita, I can't even imagine. Having to get all your sources correct and citing everything correctly."

"It is indeed. And they are very strict about adhering to scholarly sources."

"How much longer until you complete the program?

"Another year. If I go back."

Kate leans against the front seat and asks, "What gives, Vita?"

"Let's get checked in then we'll talk. Okay?"

"Fair enough," she says and leans back in her seat.

As I pull in front of the office Kate says, "Stay in the car, love. I'll check us in." Then she hops out and walks gracefully, clutch in hand, into the office.

Why did I tell her about school? Damn, I don't want to talk about that tonight. Well, there really is no better person to confide in about this.

My eyes are fixed on Kate as I watch her head from the office back to the car and then she hop's in the front passenger seat. She gives me a big smile and I grin and say, "Obviously, we are officially off-duty now, correct?"

"We are indeed!" She says with a big smile. I just look at her and keep her gaze and enjoy her beautiful smile.

I give her a slow body glance and say, "Hmmm, I like you up here next to me." Then I give her a wink and put the car in drive as she laughs at me. Hearing her own personal laugh makes me happy. This is a different side than the public gets. I love them both, but this side of her personality is only for those who are close to her.

"Our Villa is three down from this one," Kate says as she points over to the right. 'Our Villa,' I repeat in my head. We are sharing a room? I swallow hard trying to keep the butterflies in. I don't say a word, I just pull up to what looks to be a seagreen stucco bungalow and smile.

Kate says, "Come on, let's get our luggage so we can head to the beach. I glance at her and she is already climbing out of the car before I have time to pull the key out. I"ve never seen her so elated.

Just as I grab the keys I hear my door open and see Kate standing smiling at me. "I thought it was my turn to open your door, ma'am," she says while smiling at me. I just look up at her and grin.

Stepping out I stand within inches of her face and whisper, "Well, thank you Miss Kennedy. Aren't you quite the lady." She meets my eyes with her confident demeanor then shuts the door while still grinning at me.

CHAPTER FIVE: KATE

Vita and I walk into the living room of our Villa. I immediately open the double french doors and feel the coastal breeze as we step out into the sand that is only a few feet from our door.

"Oh Kate, this is amazing."

"Yes, it is, Vita. Smell that lovely cool, misty aroma, love."

"It smells incredible, I'm going to change into a warm cardigan and capris, sweetheart. What about you?"

Glancing at her I see her gazing at me and I whisper, "You just called me sweetheart."

Vita catches my fingers with hers and softly asks, "Is that okay?"

I immediately intertwine my fingers with hers and look out into the darkness and see the moonlight riding the ocean waves. My heart is full of love for this woman. I glance back at her and whisper, "Yes, Vita. It's more than okay."

I gaze into those same brooding dark eyes that enchanted me last Friday as she sat on her Motorcycle and quoted Kierkegaard. As I look at her in the seaside moonlight I realize just how much I want her, but I don't know if I am allowed to have her or not. There are a million reasons why this shouldn't happen so I release her hand and say, "Yes, I have something to wear. Let's change, okay?" Vita smiles at me and nods.

As I undress in my bedroom I begin to rethink the decision I made at the office when I checked us in. I had the gentleman exchange the two room cabins for a two bedroom villa, I must tell Vita this. I didn't even ask her. Damn, that was unfair, I should have asked.

As I walk back out onto the sand just outside our door I see Vita. She's wearing a dark cardigan and white capri pants. The night breeze catches her dark curls as I watch her looking out toward the water. She is so beautiful. Vita glances at me over her shoulder. I see her sweet smile, but I don't return it.

"What's wrong, Kate?"

Nodding my head I tell her. "Vita, I exchanged our two room cabins for this Villa to share without consulting you. I'm sorry. I should have asked you first."

She laughs. "Kate, are you serious?"

I don't know if I should laugh or not.

Vita grabs my hand and says, "Hush, woman, and walk with me."

I begin to laugh knowing it's obviously okay with her. "Let me shut these doors."

Closing the doors I hear Vita laughing and yelling, "Now you have to catch me."

Running after her I begin to laugh with renewed energy at this incredible young woman, "Vita! Wait!"

She laughs all the way to the water as I watch the moonlight reflecting on her white capris that are almost submerged in the ocean. Vita raises her hands high above her head and spins around.

I stop and gaze at her and think. How could I not love this woman?

"Come on, Kate! It's cold, but exhilarating as hell!"

I begin to laugh. Vita asks, "What are you laughing at?"

"You! Life! The beach! All of it!"

Vita steps away from the water, slowly making her way towards me. I feel her velvety eyes on me. Though it's too dark to see them clearly, I sense them. She approaches until we're mere inches apart, locking her gaze with mine. Her hand reaches for my cheek, gently drawing me closer. Vita's lips are cool and tender, tasting of moonlight and sea salt. The kiss is sweet and brief, yet full of her intentions for me.

Vita then takes my hand and says, "Come on, sweetheart, let's walk."

We walk hand in hand down the moonlit beach, watching the wave crash and exchanging intimate glances.

We make it back inside the living area leaving the french doors wide open to continue enjoying the night breeze and hear the waves break.

'That walk was refreshing," Vita says joyfully.

"Yes it was, love. It was rejuvenating!" I say then run quickly to the bathroom to grab a towel. As I smile and laugh I begin drying Vita off. "Look at you, your pants are soaked." She just laughs at me.

"Well, I'll just take them off," she says as she begins undressing.

"That's probably the best idea, I'll never get them dry with this lightweight towel." Watching Vita undress moves me sensually, I can't help but wait to gaze at what was beneath those tight khakis she wore last Friday. Looking at her lovely, smooth legs that only the moonlight and I are peeping at, my yearning for her increases. She looks at me knowing I'm admiring her gentle curves and the strength of her gorgeous legs.

"I better go put on my pajama pants," she says softly before she turns to leave. Reaching for her hand I whisper, "Wait…please."

Our fingers intertwine, and then Vita says, "Kate, let me put my pajama pants on, and then we'll talk, okay?"

I nod at her, knowing she is right. She smiles at me, then kisses my cheek before leaving for her room. Walking to my room I choose to put my pajamas on as well. Shaking my head I know I'm the one making this difficult for both of us. My affection and desire for her has been swift and almost overpowering these last two days. The fire that ignited last Friday is beginning to burn faster and hotter, and I'm the one who's fanning it the most. I know I must reel myself in, but it's so damn hard; Vita's allure has me captivated.

Vita is sitting in one of the Adirondack chairs with her legs pulled up and heels on the edge of the chair. She smiles at me as I sit beside her in the other chair. Things are silent for a few moments as we listen to the night waves washing peacefully onto the sand.

"Well, Vita, should we talk about school or perhaps something else."

Vita looks over at me and says, "School issues can wait, Kate. Our feelings for one another can't."

Gazing at the water I start the conversation. "Vita, you have been a complete professional….

"Kate, sweetheart, I know. We are beyond that. We must talk about our feelings and our intentions before this wild-fire gets out of hand."

"Wow, Vita, you pegged that, precisely."

Vita reaches for my hand and I gladly offer it to her. She leans in and kisses my hand as she peers into my soul. "Kate, I want this, I want you, there is no denying that, sweetheart."

Smiling at her I whisper, "And I want you, Vita. I've been telling myself there are a million reasons why this shouldn't happen, but none are valid enough to throw this away. It's too special. You're too special, Vita."

"Yes, Kate. I imagine it's my age, your career, not to mention your relationship with Grandma."

"Those are only a few, love."

"What are the reasons why this should happen, Kate?"

"Oh, Vita, my love. There are a billion reasons why I want you."

"Kate, I have fallen hard for you. I had a terrible crush on you in my early teenage years when I lived in Savannah, before Dad passed away. By the time I was seventeen, I knew I loved you, but what I feel for you isn't a teenage crush. I am twenty-eight years old, Kate. I've been in love and had my heart broken, so I know what love is and what it isn't."

"Vita, you're a very mature woman. The age is a bit troubling, but only because of Hazel, I believe."

"Kate, Grandma doesn't run my life, you know that."

"I do, Vita, but she runs mine, in so many ways."

"Then we will have to figure out a way to make her understand."

We continue holding hands and peer out at the moonlight reflecting on the waves. As I glance at Vita, she turns her head to me, and I bring her hand to my lips; I kiss it gently while gazing into those deep brown eyes of hers. "Vita, I've fallen hard for you as well, baby."

"I have spent the last fifteen years mostly alone because the women I've been with didn't want to live hidden in my spotlight."

"And how would that be different for us? For me, Kate?"

"That's a damn good question, love. But, a question I am mature enough to face now. I know we haven't really begun a relationship, so if you need to walk away now, then I will understand."

"Hmmm, so you would understand if I just walked away?

Really?" Vita asks while looking at me with a disconcerted look.

I stand and lean against the door casing. Then I begin lightly kicking the sand with my feet thinking about her question. I glance over my shoulder and look down at her still sitting in the chair waiting on my reply.

"Hell, no, Vita. I wouldn't understand how you could walk away honestly. I guess those are words that I've scored on my heart when things got too tough in past relationships."

I lean my back against the door casing, cross my arms, and say, "If you fled Vita, I'd follow you into hell, catch you, and then bring you back to me even if you were kicking and screaming."

Vita jumps out of her chair and grabs me around my neck. I wrap my arms around her waist laughing at her in the beautiful moonlight. "Now, that's the Kate I know and love!" She says enthusiastically.

Looking into those velvety eyes as we laugh I say "And I love you, Vita." Then I look at my young love who has just professed her love for me. I feel young and free with this woman. She gives me hope and joy. "You make me feel so alive, my sweet Vita."

We stand holding one another, our faces inches apart, our eyes interlocked communicating our love for one another. I pull back a bit to look at Vita's lips. She leans in and whispers softly in my ear, "You may kiss them Miss Kennedy."

Grinning with anticipation I glance back at her and say, "Vita, you are a pure delight, my love." Then she leans in to meet me as our lips touch one another, like a whisper in the darkness. We keep our kisses soft and gentle, easing gently into our romance with one another.

～

The next morning my bed is moving and jerking as I wake. I open my eyes and see that Vita has entered my bedroom and is jumping on my mattress like a kid. I begin laughing at her.

"Wake up, Kate!! Let's take a walk on the beach before we shower and head out. I have coffee in the kitchen." She is smiling at me as she continues jumping then quickly says, "Come on, sleepy-head." She dismounts then runs quickly towards the kitchen.

As I continue resting I begin to smile wondering how I am going to keep up with this ball of energy. I quickly throw the covers back knowing full well I can match her energy.

Entering the kitchen I say, "Well, good-morning, love."

Vita walks slowly to me and whispers, "I need a morning kiss."

I grab and encircle her waist and ask, "And where might you find one of those so early?" I ask with a sensual whisper.

She places her arms around my neck, giggles, and then gently presses her tender, soft lips against mine. Vita feels incredible in my arms and against my lips. The same gentleness from last night has ushered in a new day. "Damn, woman," I say.

Vita laughs then says, "Here's your coffee, sweetheart."

"Thank you, love." I say as I sip my coffee then wink at her. "You look adorable in these pajamas."

"I do, huh?"

"Yeah, huh. You do." I say then laugh.

We are both so giddy with love for one another. I grab her hand and walk us over to the open doors and peer out at the morning waves, and the seagulls scurrying about.

"I hate to leave this, Kate,"

"Well, we are traveling basically up the entire coastal highway. We won't be far away from the beach."

"That's not it, Kate," She says, still holding my hand sipping her coffee.

I gaze at her and smile, "I understand, Vita."

"Last night was magical, Kate. Walking with you on the beach, then hearing those three lovely words from your heart. I just don't want to leave."

I nod at her, "Neither do I, baby."

"Kate?"

"Yes?

"Let's sit for a moment. Okay?"

"Well, sure."

We both sit in the same chairs as last night and then Vita turns towards me. I take a sip of coffee as I wait for her to speak. "Kate, today I am your driver and assistant again. I want to keep my head on straight. I know since last night, we are beyond this, however, for the benefit of the tour and your protection I am going to retreat a bit, sweetheart."

"You do mean temporarily, don't you?"

"Oh course I mean temporarily you gorgeous woman."

I laugh at her, smile and nod. "I agree, Vita. And you have been professional and amazing. If anything, I'm the one who has forgotten about all my engagements. As I told you last night, I have fallen hard for you, Vita. And that's mostly all I've wanted to focus on, but you're right. Thank you, love."

"You're welcome, sweetheart. Now I know we can't stuff the genie back in the bottle, nor do I want to. However, we must try and maintain more of a platonic relationship especially in front of others."

"Okay, Vita, then we are back on the tour and my engagements. But let me tell you this."

"Sure, go ahead."

"When we finish in New York and head back to Savannah......"

"Yes?"

"You belong to me Vita St. John. OK?!"

Vita, gives me a huge grin and those velvety eyes begin to

sparkle and dance for me. "You better damn well believe it, Kate Kennedy."

"Great! Then let's have that walk on the beach, shower and dress, and then head toward Norfolk, Virginia. What do you say?

"Sure thing, Boss," Vita says then snickers.

We both laugh as we jump up and head to the water to soak in some morning sunshine and happiness.

CHAPTER SIX: VITA

The last three days and nights with Kate have been amazing. We have kept our commitment to maintaining a professional atmosphere when we are in public. Not so much so when we are alone. Despite keeping separate lodging arrangements in cabins or rooms the past two nights, our yearning for one another has made it unbearable at times.

We are still sharing intense glances and soft brief kisses each night before bedtime and every morning with our coffee. However, we are both committed to finishing this promotional tour before we delve deeper into this relationship.

We just left Washington D.C. and are on our way to Baltimore Maryland. It's just a two hour drive so we will have a bit more time today to breathe and perhaps share some time alone.

I glance into my rearview mirror to catch a glimpse of my lovely Kate. She is looking out her window and seems to be in deep thought. "What ya thinking about, gorgeous?"

"Oh, Vita. Your flattery is spoiling me."

"Good, you should be spoiled."

"Vita, I was actually thinking of you."

"Hmmm, tell me your thoughts."

"I was thinking we have a couple of hours until we reach Baltimore so I was hoping you would tell me why you're thinking of not finishing your masters program."

"Oh, that. Well, perhaps I should be more careful about asking what's on your mind," I say before laughing.

"As you well know, that night in Wilmington took a romantic turn, so we never discussed it. And I've been sitting back here for two days without you bringing it up, so I thought I would ask."

I glance back at Kate and see those vexing gray eyes waiting for a logical response to her question. "Well, sweetheart, I took classes over the summer, as you know. Butted heads with one of my professors, as I told you before. So, my hot-headed self told him what I thought of his religious theories right before I told him to 'go to hell.'"

"Then I packed my bags, sent them on a Greyhound bus to Grandma's. Hopped on my Indian Scout, leaving tire marks on the asphalt at Emory College after my temper had gotten the better of me. Then I ended up in Savannah the next day."

"That was quite a vivid scene you just described, love. Perhaps you should think about, "taking up a pen," Vita.

"I actually have, Kate," I say as my eyes search for hers in the mirror again.

"You have?! Well, baby, that's great. But you know having that masters degree sure would give you a leg up in your future. Especially since you're a female."

'That's true, Kate."

"What are you writing, Vita?"

"It's mostly rambling at the moment but I am thinking of titling it, *The Creator Within: Exploring God and the Individual.*"

"Interesting title, Vita. I sense Kierkegaard's influence in that title. Who is your audience?"

"Well, so far, it's just me. I've struggled to connect with others who prioritize their personal beliefs over the teachings of the church as well as their spiritual journey with our creator."

"I believe you have two readers now, my love." Kate sweetly says to me.

Glancing back at Kate I say, "Thank you, sweetheart."

"Vita, I'm serious. That's exactly what I believe."

"Really. I mean, I have felt it in your writing, but I wasn't sure."

"Love, much of my material derives from our creator. I couldn't possibly have written thirteen books without God's influence. When I am writing though I have to be careful not to get heavy-handed when speaking about God. Most people don't realize that God is their source. The fountain-head. So I have to guise it into Self-Help talk that makes more sense to them."

"Wow, sweetheart, that's impressive." I glance back at Kate and see her gazing out the window again. I begin to marvel and wonder what goes on in that gorgeous head of hers. Damn, beauty and brains. You don't find that often.

"Vita, find us a place for lunch. Okay?"

"Would love to, I'm hungry. Hey here's a place up ahead. The sign has a big cow sitting on top. You think we could find a burger there?"

Kate bursts into laughter, "Oh, Vita. You're a damn mess!"

"I might indulge today. I mean since you've basically said you're mine, then it doesn't matter how fat I get now."

Kate continues laughing at me. "Oh, hell yes, it does. I want to see you in those khaki pants again, and those sexy boots, strutting up my sidewalk like you did last Friday."

"You watched me walk up your sidewalk that day, Kate Kennedy?!"

"You bet your sweet pretty ass I did. You kicked me in the gut when you dismounted your bike with that tousled hair. Then you strutted all the way up my sidewalk, and into my heart, Vita St. John."

I roar with laughter, "Kate!!" Why haven't you said anything?!"

"Hell, Vita, I thought you'd figured it out. Woman, I was like a cat in heat by the time you showed me your motorcycle, quoted Kierkegaard, and then sped off, leaving me standing on the sidewalk."

"Oh, Kate, sweetheart." I pull into the restaurant parking far away from the other cars. I put the car in park and then look down as I hold my fist against my mouth, trying my best not to cry.

Kate gets out of the back seat immediately and in a flash she is in the front seat next to me. "Vita, my love. It's okay, baby. I meant to make you laugh, not cry. But I also wanted you to know what you've done to me. Vita, I'm crazy about you."

I keep my fist tight against my mouth and nod. She is sitting quietly holding my arm with both of her hands. "I'm okay now, sweetheart. And I've definitely fallen for you too, Kate."

"Oh, Vita, my love. That makes me incredibly happy." She looks at me tenderly and then says, "Come on. Let's go have that burger. A few more curves on that lovely body would actually make me even crazier about you."

"Oh Hush, woman!"

"Are you sure you're okay?" She asks sweetly.

"Yes, you just threw me. My gosh what a picture you painted of me and how it made you feel. Sweetheart, It was funny indeed, but I had no idea that you went that ga-ga over me." I look at Kate and grin, "I don't even know what to say to that."

Kate kisses my hand briefly and winks at me and whispers, "Well, now you know how you made me feel that day."

I nod at her then open my car door and exit. We walk toward the restaurant in laughter. "You're unreal, Kate." She smiles at me as she puts her arm around my shoulder then gives me a quick wink before we reach the entrance. Then she catches my eyes and opens the front door for me. "You make me feel like Cinderella, Kate, Kennedy."

"Oh Vita, my love, you are far meatier and grittier than Cinderella could ever hope to be." I burst into laughter all the way through the entrance.

"Are you sure you're okay to drive, Vita? It's been a long day and it's about two hours to Wilmington, Delaware.

"Of course I am. That's not long. Plus that means we won't have to get up early and drive in the morning."

"Yes, I am going to enjoy sleeping in, that's for sure. Oh, and we will stay two nights in Wilmington, thank goodness. Hazel always works in a two night stay when possible."

"Kate, you have completed about twenty of your engagements so far."

"I know, thank-goodness. We are winding down, love. We'll be in New York City in a couple of days."

"Take a nap, sweetheart," I say to her.

Kate grabs her travel pillow, pitches it on the seat then stretches out. "Thank you, I believe I will close my eyes for a while."

With complete contentment and a grin I continue our drive to Wilmington, sneaking a quick glance back at my sleeping beauty from time-to-time.

It's dark but I think I see the sign, *Riverview lodge.* As I turn in I see Kate sit up in the back seat. I smile.

"Are we here, love?"

"Yes we are here, indeed. How was your nap?"

"Unsettling, I had a bad dream just before I woke."

I stop the car, put it in park, then turn to look at her. "It must have shook you, sweetheart. You sound quite somber."

"I'm okay. Thank you. I'll go inside and check us in."

"Wait right there, Kate."

I walk around to her door and open it, she looks up at me and gives me a smile. "Thank you, Vita. This is sweet."

"I'm here to take care of you, sweetheart." Kate gets out and stands within inches of my face like she has done so many times on this trip.

"Vita, you do indeed take great care of me, my love," she whispers. Then gently grasps my hand and gives me a sweet smile. I hold her eyes briefly before I shut her door.

"Let's go check in, okay?" I nod and give her a wink.

As we enter the office of the hotel we are greeted by a kind older lady with short dark hair. "Good Evening ladies. My name is Mary, do you have reservations?"

Kate begins to give her our information, telling her that we have two rooms. I quickly decide to interject. "Mary, Miss Kennedy and I need these next two evenings to discuss her remaining engagements on her promotional tour."

Mary gives me a perplexed look. I don't look at Kate for her reaction I just move forward saying, "Would you perhaps be able to exchange our two individual rooms with one that has two bedrooms? This way we will be able to effectively plan out the next few days."

Looking at Kate I see her sucking in her cheeks like she did once before when she didn't think I noticed. She gives me a small grin and then turns to Mary and says, "Yes, Mary, that would be most helpful. Could you do that?"

Mary remains silent as she flips through her registry book. I give Kate a quick glance and notice that she is about to break into sweet laughter. I furrow my brow and nod quickly, then notice her sucking in those adorable cheeks again. She turns and walks to the postcard rack and begins flipping through them, picks one out, and lays it on the desk.

"Yes I can," says Mary.

I want to give Mary a hug, but I remain calm and I don't look at Kate again. Glancing at her a moment ago was a bad idea.

Laying a nickel on the desk for the postcard Kate whispers, "Thank you, Vita."

Mary gives us our key and then we are back in the car and begin to roar with laughter. "Miss Kennedy, you need to work on your Poker-Face!" I say with laughter.

"Hell, Vita! Next time warn a girl!" Our laughter fills the car as we drive to reach our room. I park the car in front of our motel room door, turn off the car, then turn my head around towards Kate.

"Is it okay that I switched rooms without consulting you?" I ask with a giggle.

"Vita, you are full of surprises, love. And yes, it's definitely okay. Come on, let's get inside."

I jump out with excitement knowing Kate will be so close to me. These last few nights with her in a different motel room has been necessary, but they have also been excruciatingly lonely. This may be a bad idea, but I want her near me.

"Oh look, Vita. We have a lovely small living area here with sliding french doors. Kate opens them and I join her immediately on the deck that overlooks the Delaware River. Standing beside Kate she takes my hand, our fingers interlock. Her touch is both calming and exhilarating. "This is so lovely, and we will be here two full nights, my love."

I glance up at her and meet her gaze. Kate brings my hand

to her lips and kisses it sweetly and then closes her eyes, smelling my hand. How did we happen? This is completely magical. I glance around to see if anyone is nearby. No one is out so I encircle Kate from behind and hold her tight against me. She leans her head back letting it rest against mine. Then I whisper, "I love you."

Kate turns toward me, gives me a tender look and then places her hands on my cheeks and whispers, 'And I love you, Vita."

We walk back inside, leaving the doors open to watch the moonlight sparkle on the peaceful river. Reaching to turn the lamp on Kate says, "Vita, wait…" I glance back at her and she is walking towards me. She reaches for my cheeks again and brings me to her giving me an intense and passionate kiss, our hungry tongues finally meet one another. Tongues that were once strangers are now intimately entangled. I reach around her shoulders and Kate grabs me around my waist and pulls me to her. Our zealous kisses are feral and uncontrollable. This woman knows how to kiss, and her passion for me is evident. I grip her loose curls of blond hair and hold them tight letting her know she is mine. Kate moans, then brings one hand up to my hair and grips it with complete dominance.

It's clear that we are both strong women, each seeking to assert ourselves for the other, yet doing so with deep affection and tender passion. Both wanting to please the other, yet grasping to quench our own hunger as well. We break away, but pull one another close, "My god, Vita. I can't stand another day, another minute not knowing you fully."

She pulls away and looks at me to read my face. I look at her and grin and whisper, "Kate, I've been in agony these last few nights, I can't stand it any longer either. Close those doors and lock them, sweetheart."

CHAPTER SEVEN: KATE

Vita meets me in the bedroom and I pull her close and whisper, "Are you sure you're okay with this, love?"

She nods at me and softly says, "I know everything will change after this, Kate. But I am ready if you are, sweetheart."

"Vita, I am more than ready. I've been in undeniable pain for you. Gazing at your lovely curls from the back seat the last several days has driven me quite mad."

Vita laughs then whispers, "Kate, I know we are both starving for one another, but let's take it slow and tender for a while. We have all night. Is that okay, sweetheart?"

I nod at her. "Yes, baby, of course." I'll take this young beautiful woman any way she offers herself to me. Vita begins undressing me slowly as I just stand and gaze into her eyes with my fingers in those dark lovely curls. Her dark brooding eyes have me hypnotized. I'll do anything she wishes.

My hunger wants to ravish this young woman and feel her fight back with her own loving passionate strength. But, I don't, instead I relinquish the reins to this lovely creature, allowing her to guide us into the depths of our erotic voyage.

Continuing to watch her unbutton my blouse I smile at her then give her a gentle kiss on those sweet tender lips. "I love you, Vita."

I draw back and gaze at the catchlights reflecting in Vita's beautiful dark eyes, illuminated by the shimmering moonlight that fills our bedroom. Vita removes my blouse and then looks at my cleavage and nods her head slowly giving me a playful grin. "I love you too, Miss Kennedy."

I grin at her. "Oh Vita."

"Yes, Kate?"

"I look at her intensely and say there's more, Vita?'

She looks oddly at me and repeats, "More?"

'Yes…much more. I touch her cheek and gaze at her and softly say, "Vita St. John, I am completely and hopelessly in love with you."

Vita reaches around my neck giving me her whole body to love. Never, have I felt this in love in my life. I want this woman with every cell I am composed of. Every dream I've ever wished for is so minuscule compared to how I wish for this woman in my arms. I embrace and hold her tighter than I've ever held anything. My strength grows and I feel as though I might crush her with this overflowing love I feel.

My hand travels inside her pants searching for her ass to curb my strength. I find it and then grab it with my hand. The strength that was embracing her has found a temporary quiet release. Vita's ass is soft and full making me hungry for more. Hell, if all she offered me tonight was this sweet ass I'd gladly take it and be happy.

Vita pulls away and says, "Miss Kennedy. You, sit down. Now." I laugh, and then do as I'm told. Sitting on the bed I wait on her as she undresses for me.

"Since you obviously can't behave Miss Kennedy, you will

have to wait until I am completely undressed before you may touch me again."

"Vita! You are so naughty. Making me wait."

"It's your own fault, sweetheart." Vita says, then giggles at me.

I reach for her but she jumps away. "Stop that, or I'll punish you severely."

"Vita, my gosh. You're unreal."

"Well, I ask you nicely to take things slow, but you disobeyed me."

Laughing loudly I lean back on the bed and watch this seductive motorcycle riding vixen tame my ass. I just keep grinning as she slowly undresses for me. And I mean slowly. Doesn't she know I am dying. Well, hell of course she does. This little tease is going to pay for this after she releases me from detention.

"Take your clothes off, Miss Kennedy." I jump up knowing I am free again and finish undressing as I look at Viita's incredibly erotic body full of heavenly curves.

"Your ass is divine, Vita St. John."

"Yes, I know. I get that quite often," She says then grins at me.

"Hmmm, you do? Well, it's my ass now, so the others best back away."

"So, you're that possessive?" She asks, wanting to hear me say yes.

"Vita, I've never been accused of being possessive...until now. But now, I must confess, it's true. I'm incredibly posses-sive of you, love."

Sitting back on the bed I wait for my love to come to me and I'll gladly take her slowly just as she requests. She walks her lovely nude body towards me and then stops before she reaches me and softly says, "Kate, you are such a gorgeous woman. Your body is even more beautiful than in my fantasies. Gazing at you is making me weak."

"Come here, and I'll hold you, love." I pull Vita to me and into my lap holding her tenderly. Our eyes meet and I feel love, lust, and contentment in great abundance.

"Let's get in bed, sweetheart." Vita whispers.

We pull the covers back and get into bed, our hungry bodies meeting in the middle. Lying on our sides, I pull her close, and we gaze at each other by moonlight that streams through the large window. Vita is right, this is too special to rush. We proceed with tenderness and gentleness, treating each other as if we might break.

Vita's warm body merges with mine, and we become one, seeking to know each other intimately and spiritually. "Oh Vita," I whisper between soft, deep kisses.

"I love everything about you, Kate," Vita pulls away briefly to look at me. "Kate, I knew one day you would be mine. Somehow I just knew it, sweetheart. During my young teenage years I had an awful crush on you. And as I entered my late teenage years I knew that I loved you, and you were never far from my thoughts. Friday when I drove to your home…" She pauses for a moment.

"What, Vita?"

"I wasn't there to see Grandma, Kate. I came to Savannah to claim you. Knowing that I am a grown woman, fully capable of loving you the way you deserve. As I walked up the sidewalk to your house, my entire goal was to show you that I'm a mature Vita now. I wanted to make you see me in a completely new light."

"Kate, you consumed my thoughts the whole ride from Atlanta to Savannah on my motorcycle. I knew I wanted you, and it was damn time that I let you know."

My heart feels as though it might explode, I'm speechless. I feel a tear. An unfamiliar wetness weeps from my eyes. "My god, Vita. I don't even know how to respond to that, baby. But how did you know?"

"Kate, sweetheart, look at me and be honest, okay?"

"Yes, of course, my love."

"The last time I saw you about ten years ago I felt the magic between us then. Did you?

"Vita, you were such a very young woman then honey. I couldn't allow my thoughts to delve too deeply about what I felt for you."

Vita looks at me with those same velvety eyes I fell for years ago, but I've been too ashamed to admit it, even to myself. The tears are growing so I know she has every right to know the truth. I nod and say, "Yes, Vita. I wanted you then, but it hurts admitting it to you."

"Why, Kate?"

"Vita, honey you were barely eighteen…." I pause. "Vita, yes, I have to be honest with you, baby." I look into the same dark eyes I've watched grow from a young teenager into this vibrant and sensual woman who now shares my bed.

"Yes, Vita. I wanted you then and I did indeed fantasize about making love to you many nights. You have lived inside of me for years, Vita."

Vita touches my face as we gaze at one another, faces inches apart. "Thank you, Kate. I needed to hear that from you. I don't know why, perhaps I needed to know that this fire has burned from both sides through the years."

"It has, Vita. You are a strong woman. My god, you're amazing and relentless. I love how you hold my feet to the fire, it's sexy as hell. I turn my head and lay my arm on my forehead as I look up at the ceiling.

I whisper, "Yes, my sweet Vita, I have loved you for years."

Vita touches my cheek pulling me back to her. I see her lovely smile and the incredible love she has for me. She then rises up and I meet her eyes again as she gives me a grin and a seductive wink.

I grab Vita in my arms and move on top of her giving her deep lustful kisses full of my passion for her. Our tongues entangle with intensity, and I feel her matching my desire, signaling a transition into the next stage. It feels amazing as I release my pent up desire for her. Showing her that yes, I am indeed possessive of her and that she has been mine forever. I'm possessive of this ass, as I grab it, these breasts that fill my hands. I'm possessive of everything, of every breath she breathes. "You are mine, Vita, and you always have been." I say with complete confidence.

"Yes, Kate. And you belong to me, I claim you." She whispers back as she grabs my hair. I begin moving my body between her legs. The same glorious legs that strutted up my driveway to show herself to me will soon be parted. To hold, to push apart, to enjoy with all my strength. I work my way to her breasts, grasping them firmly, but with love. I kiss them, suck them, and I love them.

I look up and see those dark eyes gazing at me, so I watch them. I watch how she responds as I lick her nipple with the tip of my tongue. Vita whimpers.

Moving to her sexual mound I smell her. My god, she smells like the good earth mingled with her youthful clean aroma. It evokes the memory of the sea salt from the shoreline, where she first kissed me. "Take me, Kate." She whispers.

I'm loving how Vita responds to my touch, to my mouth, lips and tongue. All of my senses are in complete union as I enjoy this unique and complex woman. Vita parts her legs for me, then I kiss her sweet and tender clit. "Oh, Kate, yes."

My tongue continues tasting and feeling Vita's womanness. She is indeed a mature woman now who is fully capable of loving me, possessing me, taming me. I want to consume

Vita's feminine essence. I suck, lick and love every inch of her sweetness as I feel her clit grow increasingly hard for me as it swells.

Vita rises up, our mouths meet as I share her sweet nectar. She licks my mouth, then grips my hair and pushes her hungry tongue deep inside my mouth and it searches for its mate. I feel my love for vita as I grab her, pulling her to me forcefully. Vita moves on top of me, never releasing my mouth as she climbs onto my lap.

Damn, Vita is unreal. She is indeed an alpha woman, just as I am. I already know that our fights will be like fireworks, but I don't give a damn. I proceed with my unwavering lust to possess and explore this splendid woman who has been mine forever.

Vita rises to her knees. I find her wetness with my finger tips. Then I gather some of her delicious liquid onto my fingers. I enter her deep and strong. In one complete swift movement I thrust into Vita's heavenly abyss.

Our mouth's have yet to release, and I won't let go until it's time for her to cry out for me in sweet elation. As I thrust into Vita she grabs my hair with her fists, bracing herself for a ride that she wants and needs. We are both whimpering and moaning as I thrust relentlessly into Vita. Taking her. Making her mine. Forever.

I feel Vita tighten around my fingers, she's squeezing them and it feels incredible. I clutch her soft curls and then give her all of my strength hitting her core with sharp and intentional thrusts. It's been forever since I've had a woman. But Vita isn't just a woman, she is my young radiant goddess who is allowing me the privilege to love her.

Vita's mouth releases mine and our eyes lock, reminding me of that day on the sidewalk when they met after many years apart. But today, I won't be shamed into releasing them. No, today I claim them as they allow me to watch her lose herself to me.

"Yes, Vita, come baby. I'll catch you." Her eyes go soft as does her expression. I watch my love, the one I've loved forever lose herself to me as we have both wanted for years.

"Kate. My beautiful, Kate," she whispers to me as she looks deep inside me. I hold onto her soft loose curls allowing her to let go and fall through her beautiful orgasm. My lovely Vita, my brave and strong woman.

Vita closes those dark eyes, she is still climaxing, I can feel her. I continue my forceful thrust as I enjoy watching my beautiful woman freefall with eyes closed. "Yes, love," I whisper as I feel the end coming. She moans and then falls against me, and I leave my fingers deep inside her. "Oh Vita. I love you, and yes, I've loved you forever."

CHAPTER EIGHT: VITA

As I lie against Kate I feel her immense love for me. "That was the most beautiful orgasm I've ever had, Kate." She hugs me tight as I feel her gently pull out of me. She then moves on top of me and gazes into my eyes. I smile into her vexing gray eyes that I've loved since I've known her.

As she gazes at me, I softly say, "I feel like I've been in love with you my entire life, Kate." She nods in response, her eyes tenderly locked with mine.

"I feel the same way, Vita. And I will never feel ashamed of it again, because you are my greatest gift."

I wrap my arms tightly around her neck and then kiss her softly, fingers intertwined in her lovely blonde locks of hair. "You're an amazing lover, Kate. I knew you would be."

"Vita, all I did was give you everything in me. All the love and passion I've felt for you for years." I smile at her as I fight back the tears. Finally, Kate Kennedy is mine, completely all mine. I sigh with contentment.

Determined to show this woman my passion for her, I

grip her tightly. And then in one forceful swift movement I'm on top of her gaining possession of her.

"Damn, Vita," she says with a laugh. "You are the most beautiful and dominant woman that has ever crossed my path, love. How in the hell did you gain all of this sexy confidence?"

"From reading your books, sweetheart."

Kate roars with laughter, "My Books?! Vita, you're such a breath of freshness in my stale life! You can't learn what you have from books, Vita St. John. Honey, this is something you were born with."

I can't help but join her in laughter, her sweet and charming laugh that lights my heart. "Well, maybe that's what I should write a book about. What ya think?"

"Yes, honey. Flush your other book and name this one…" She pauses, Then says, "Vita St. John: Embracing Confidence and Swagger."

Falling off of her and onto the bed I scream with laughter, "Kate. Oh gosh." I can't control my laughter. And in my weakness Kate has taken advantage of me. She is back on top of me holding me down as she laughs with me.

"You like that title, Vita?"

"Oh my god, you're unreal, Kate." I gaze at her loveliness as my laughter subsides.

After our laughter dissipates I feel the sexual tension again and my longing to show this woman my love and erotic passion that has lived in me for years.

Seductively I whisper, "What would you like from me, sweetheart?"

"Oh Vita," she whispers as I reach down to find her sex. Kate rises up a bit allowing me to reach her. I grip the back of her hair and then begin rubbing her clit with soft circles. I reach further to grab her liquid then move back to her clit. Our eyes are locked as I watch her begin to submit to me.

"You like this, sweetheart?" I ask softly. She nods then closes her pretty eyes for a bit. I continue feeling her softness as I watch her lovely face. My older woman, my lover, whom I would die for. Suddenly, I stop my movements and ease out beneath her. Standing beside the bed I look at Kate who has a curious, but provocative look on her face.

I whisper, "Kate, please sit on the edge of the bed for me." As she moves to where I ask, I kneel on the floor in front of her. I'm between Kate's legs and I gaze up at her and see her smile. "I've waited a lifetime to taste you, sweetheart. And now I desire full access to you."

"Oh, Vita," she whispers. How did I win your love? Your pure, unapologetic love."

She touches my cheeks and then softly says, "I'm all yours, Vita. Take me, my young lover."

With that she leans back resting her elbows on the bed and pulls those sensual long legs apart for me. I remain where I am gazing at the strength of her legs, the smoothness and the maturity of them. My eyes rest on hers and I continue loving her legs with my hands, caressing them. Her eyes grow curious, I feel it. She is wondering how I am going to feel loving her.

Holding her legs, I break our gaze as I lower my mouth to her intimate feminine center. I smell her…. Finally, I smell the woman I've loved forever. I whisper, "Oh, please help me Kate, you smell incredible. I've waited forever to know your scent."

All I want to do is just breathe her in and consume this rich aroma. I feel Kate's fingers in my hair, playing with my curls. Nothing in my life has ever felt like this. No other woman I've touched or smelled could have ever broken my deep desire and the longing I've held for this woman. I want to please her, but I just want to worship this incredible woman.

As I push her legs further she opens for me allowing my mouth to taste what I've hungered for. Finally, I get to taste her forbidden fruit, the sweet fruit I wasn't allowed to taste until now.

I lap her juices onto my tongue and then listen to my saliva glands speak to me. They gently whisper, *"your obsession, taste of the dark midnight sea and a supreme rich fruit you could never find elsewhere. Taste and enjoy the woman you've ached for, she's yours now."* I hold her legs firmly and consume her, taking moments to swallow her forbidden nectar.

Kate is moaning and whispering my name as I continue to please her as well as myself. I feel her delicate and tender folds that make up her essence. I feel her swell against my tongue. "Vita, yes, my love. You feel amazing," she breathlessly says.

She is close to orgasming, however I am not finished with this once forbidden fruit so I pull away and gaze at her then whisper, "Hold off for a minute, Kate. Please." She nods at me and allows me to continue enjoying her. I suck her plump swollen clit softly then move my tongue over the top of it in back and forth movements.

"Oh, Vita. Baby I can't wait much longer."

"Sweetheart, I know." I reach underneath one leg then enter her intimate depths with my fingers as I gaze into those lovely gray eyes that I've loved my whole life. Kate shudders as I begin to pump her with my fingers finding the rhythm that sings to her. I move back to her sweet fruit as I suck and massage it, feeling its ripeness. My mouth, fingers and arm are in perfect harmony to let this lovely creature know my love.

As I continue conducting this symphony of love for her I feel her losing control. Kate grips my fingers tightly so I decide to increase the tempo, and the beat. "Vita!" She shouts. "Yes, baby, take me." Keeping at the same beat and tempo I feel her cascading, she's in a beautiful freefall. The love of my life is climaxing for me. It's emotionally fulfilling, but almost overwhelming.

"Vita. Yes, I've loved you forever, since before I was allowed to," her mouth confesses as she rides her glorious orgasm.

Kate's orgasm is long and intense as I continue the same beat and rhythm. She is reaching the end. I feel her body grow weak.

Kate sits up and grabs my face and looks into my eyes with complete tenderness and love. "Vita, my god, woman. I've never been taken like this." I smile at her. Then she grabs me, drawing me to her and whispers, "I meant what I said, I've loved you since you were too young for me to have, Vita."

"I know, Kate."

Pushing her back onto the bed I grab her bosoms and begin sucking them. Kate's full mounds have teased me the entire trip. Stealing glances of her cleavage from city to city has driven me almost insane. I'm on top of her and I suck them greedily while gazing into her eyes. Kate moans and whispers, "Heaven help me, Vita. you're incredible. Your mouth and tongue feel amazing, love."

I keep one breast cupped in my hand as my mouth continues sucking it hard. "Yes, Vita, suck it harder baby. Please." I do as she asks and suck her full perfect tits hard. Pulling at her nipples with my mouth I reach down and find her soaked sex.

I return to the same circular motions from earlier as I gaze into her eyes. Watching her face, she meets my eyes, and I can tell she is ready to fall again. This time I want to watch the woman I love lose herself as she lets go. Her gray eyes are fixed on me and I see them grow soft and peaceful as she whispers lightly, "Vita, I belong to you." I nod at her letting her know she is indeed mine. Then I bring her to orgasm, after orgasm as she gazes into my eyes with each fall.

Kate reaches her arms around me then closes those lovely long legs. "I'm spent, Vita. I can give no more, baby," she breathes.

Holding her firmly against me I smile. I think to myself Kate Kennedy is indeed mine. All mine. As I pull the covers over us I draw her to me and cradle her in my arms. We both drift off in a loving and peaceful slumber.

The sunlight floods our room with soft ambient light the following morning. Kate and I made love off and on all night long. I glance at my beautiful lover. Replaying our love-making I flash back at how she took me at 4:00 AM.

I giggle and wake her. "I'm sorry, sweetheart."

She stretches and rises onto her elbows and says, "Good morning, love. What are you giggling about?"

"Four AM sweetheart."

"Vita, my god woman, I'm an animal with you. I can't help it."

"I'm not complaining. I actually think you were tame last night. I mean, I believe there is more rawness in you that I've yet to uncover, Miss Kennedy."

"Vita, remind me what happened at 4:00 AM."

"You know damn well what happened at 4:00 AM."

Kate laughs then falls back on her pillow and says, "Perhaps."

"Perhaps, hell!" I shout at her then attempt to get out of bed, but Kate grabs me. "Sweetheart, we've got to get going. You have your first radio spot in two hours."

"You're right, love. I just want to hold you a little longer, Vita."

"Oh baby, so do I." As I snuggle next to Kate our eyes meet and I see a small tear forming. I kiss it away and then kiss her tenderly on those perfect lips.

"Vita, I love your tenderness, as well as your raw and carnal lust for me." I smile at her and nod.

"I had no idea we would be this explosive in bed, Kate. It's unbelievable."

"Neither did I, my love. But indulge me a bit before I release you."

I grin at her and ask, "How?"

"Four AM."

"Oh, I see." Kate giggles at me, but is waiting on my response. I snuggle closer and move my mouth to her ear and begin to whisper. "Hmmm, I believe you were standing at the edge of the bed. And I was on my knees on the edge of the bed with my back against those full bosoms of yours. It seems like you were holding me forcefully while you worked my clit giving me orgasm, after orgasm. Is that how you remember it, sweetheart?"

"My gosh, Vita. Yes, that's exactly how I remember that moment. Damn, woman, I'm going to cancel every event today so I can make love to you all day long."

"Kate! You better hush, or that will be a reality if we don't pry ourselves out of this bed."

Kate smiles sweetly then releases me and says, "Okay, I'll go make some coffee and you can shower first." I nod as I reluctantly rise and head to the shower. Hell, she is right. I could fuck that woman all day long, and late into night.

CHAPTER NINE: KATE

The last two days and nights with Vita have been an emotional, spiritual, and sexual awakening for me. My beautiful young lover makes me want to live fully and savor every minute of each day and night.

We spent the entire night making love again. Just as we did the night before. Pushing the boundaries of our sexual and emotional exploration. I can't get enough of Vita and have come to realize just how deeply I love her. I know that I have loved this young woman since the moment I met her. Through our lovemaking, the long-cherished fantasies have resurfaced as vivid flashbacks, compelling me to acknowledge just how deeply I craved Vita, even back then.

We're driving to Philadelphia for another day packed with radio interviews and a book signing in the late afternoon. As I sit in the back of the Packard I can't help but smile and look at those lovely curls of Vita's. The same curls I held tightly in my hands as she brought me to the edge, and held me there until she was ready to release me.

"I see you smiling, gorgeous," Vita says.

AVEN BLAIR

"Hmmm, and I bet you can imagine what I'm thinking, love."

"Oh, Kate. How did we happen, sweetheart?"

"I love you, Vita."

"And I love you, Kate."

Driving along Route 13 as the warm sun hits my eyes I suddenly hear Vita scream out with a sharp-short-cry.

"Vita! Pullover, baby!"

Opening Vita's door I see her clutching her side and crying out in pain. I begin to panic seeing my beautiful girl in so much pain. "Slide over Vita. NOW!"

I hop into the driver's seat of the Packard and hit the gas pedal, hard. "Vita, lay your head in my lap, baby." She continues crying out in pain, holding her side with her feet up on the seat. I feel her forehead—it's warm. Damn, I've got to find the closest hospital.

After receiving directions to Thomas Jefferson University Hospital, which is approximately fifteen minutes away, I urgently drive towards it, my fingers entwined in Vita's dark curls. "Vita, baby don't worry, the hospital is close."

She is in severe pain, but I can tell she is wanting to be tough for me. Holding her soft curls while searching for the hospital, I want to scream. Finally, I see it up ahead and quickly pull in front of the emergency room entrance.

"I'll be right back, Vita. Listen, sweetheart, I'm going to tell them I'm your Aunt, otherwise, they might prohibit me from seeing you. Okay?"

She whimpers, "Okay, Kate. I love you."

"I love you, Vita," I say while kissing her head. I grab my travel pillow for her then quickly get out of the car and run to the entrance to find help.

The emergency staff just accessed her and now they are loading her onto a stretcher. I hold Vita's hand as the nurse and orderly wheel her inside.

Looking at the nurse I frantically ask, "May I stay with her? I'm her Aunt."

The nurse looks at me and says, "We need to start treatment right away. It's possible that she's having an appendicitis attack."

Glancing at Vita, I want to grab her and carry her in my arms. As she looks at me she manages to give me a sweet wink that makes my heart melt. The tears fill my eyes and I give her a tender wink back.

"Ma'am you'll need to wait in the waiting area now." I lean down and kiss Vita on her soft cheek as I try hard to play the part of her concerned Aunt. I wish I could kiss her sweet lips before they take her from me. "Damn." I mumble.

As they wheel Vita away from me, it feels as though my whole world just turned dark. I pace the waiting room as my mind races on what to do. Taking a seat I glance over and see two phone booths. I know Hazel must be notified, but I don't want to call her. Vita is my love, and my responsibility now. She's my everything.

Dialing my home phone number I hear it ring and Hazel picks up.

"Hazel, this is Kate."

"Something is wrong. What's going on?"

"It's Vita. She's at the emergency room in Philadelphia. They think it's her appendix."

"Oh no! Kate, is she okay?"

"I don't know Hazel. They just took her back and they're making me wait in the waiting area."

"Kate, I am going to take the next train."

Damn, I don't want her here, but I have little choice. "Yes, Hazel. Do what you feel is right, but I'm taking care of her, and I won't leave this hospital without her."

Hazel pauses for a bit. Perhaps she picked up on my tone.

The love in my voice. Hell, I don't care. All I care about is Vita.

"What hospital, Kate?"

After I give Hazel the details of the hospital I ask her to cancel the remaining engagements on my tour. My heart is full of fear and pain as I reach the nurses reception desk.

"Yes, ma'am, how may I help you?" The receptionist asks.

"I'm Kate Kennedy and I am Vita St. Johns Aunt, will you let me know her condition as soon as you can, please?

"Yes, we will. MIss Kennedy, will you fill out these forms and give us her basic information?"

Sitting back in my seat, looking over the forms, I realize there is so much I don't know, but I fill them out as best I can. I list Vita's address as mine in Savannah. I don't know her address in Atlanta, nor do I care. Vita is mine now, and this is her address. I want this wonderful woman to live with me forever, that much I know. I put myself down as her next of kin. There is no way I am writing Hazel's name —hell no.

I hand the paperwork back to the lady and sit back down thinking of Vita and then Hazel. Hazel has a right to be here, but something is telling me this may get ugly. All I can do is sit and wait. I begin to pray and think about how much Vita told me she loved 'Our Creator' and her quest to know the nature of God. Tears flow as I pray for my sweet and beautiful love.

"Miss, Kennedy." I hear someone say loudly.

I quickly jump up and reach the desk and frantically answer, "Yes, I'm Miss Kennedy. I'm Vita's Aunt."

"It looks like they are prepping Miss St. John for surgery to perform an appendectomy."

"Is it serious? I mean I know it can be. How is she?"

"That's all I know at the moment, Miss. Kennedy."

I nod and stand at the desk hoping for more, but the lady

looks at me then says, "I promise we will let you know more as soon as possible."

I smile, nod and say, "Thank you." Then I take my seat again not knowing how my entire world flipped on its end within a couple of hours.

They brought me Vita's jacket moments ago and I immediately smelled it. Her lovely aroma from the jacket makes me want to fall on my knees and weep. I hug it tightly as if it's Vita. This jacket is all I have of her at the moment. I inhale her scent and it creates flashbacks over the last several days.

Her intoxicating scent brings up images from our trip. I see Vita devouring burgers, laughing, her lovely curls, and making love to her.

Usually always in control I find myself very vulnerable at the moment. Allowing myself to fall so deeply in love with Vita has brought up feelings that I haven't had to deal with in years.

As I sit quietly, clutching Vita's jacket, my 'black dog' of doubt creeps in. He whispers, *This is what happens when you let your guard down and become vulnerable. You can't handle this; you're not strong enough to take care of her. It's best if you leave and let Hazel care for her. Vita will be better off without you anyway.*

Under my breath I mutter, "Shut the fuck up, and leave me alone! I love this woman with everything in me and no one is taking her from me."

Covering myself with Vita's jacket It feels as though my 'black dog' has fled. Perhaps he felt my wrath. Hopefully he felt my commitment and love for Vita as well.

Closing my eyes I inhale Vita's sweet aroma from her jacket that covers and warms me. I feel close to her as I shut out the world and just breathe in her intoxicating essence and wait for any update on my beloved woman.

"Ma'am," I hear someone say. Grabbing Vita's jacket I rush to the desk.

"Yes. How is Vita?"

"She is out of surgery, but she had some complications."

I hear myself saying "Complications?" Slowly. "What do you mean?" I ask.

"Well, she had an adverse reaction to the anesthesia which has caused nausea, vomiting and severe drowsiness. The surgery is over, however, they are moving her to the critical care unit for the next several hours to monitor her."

"May I see her, Please?"

The receptionist smiles at me and says, "Visiting hours have just ended, but let me see what I can do." She leaves through a door behind her and I wait not knowing when I can see my Vita.

She returns to her desk and says, "They don't want her to have visitors until the next visiting hour, which is at 6:00 PM."

Glancing at my watch I see that it's 2:30 in the afternoon. Nodding I say, "Yes, okay. That's fine." It's not fine, but what other options do I have?

As I turn, I hear her say, "Miss Kennedy."

"Yes?" I ask.

"Why don't you go to the cafeteria and get some food, you look tired."

I smile and nod at her as I turn to go find my chair again. Pulling Vita's coat up around me I realize that I better get some food in me. I don't want anything, however, I need to keep up my strength for Vita.

As I walk to the cafeteria I calculate the time since I phoned Hazel and told her about Vita. I think it's been about five hours. Hazel will be on the next train, which will most likely put her in Philadelphia somewhere between midnight and 6:00 AM.

Looking at the selection of food in the cafeteria I see they have burgers and it makes me smile. I doubt they would be up to Vita's standards, but it still warms my heart. I opt for a salad and then sit and eat it with little enthusiasm.

I have to get a hold of myself before Hazel arrives and takes over. All I want is for Vita to get well and I know that's what Hazel wants as well. However, I can't help but feel as though this is the quiet before the storm. I know why Hazel was against Vita driving me on this promotional tour. Her suspicions were obviously right, even though that wasn't my intention—or was it?

All I know is I love Vita with every breath in me and Vita feels the same. That's what I keep clinging to. I will not allow Hazel to have too much power in my head. Vita and I are a couple, and we're in love, and she is going to have to accept that.

CHAPTER TEN: KATE

Glancing at my watch, I see it's almost time for visiting hours and I'm on edge to get to Vita. I just want to touch her, look at her, and kiss her.

As I walk behind the privacy screen to see Vita I want to cry as I hold onto her jacket. I immediately touch her forehead and notice she isn't as warm as before. Since it's just the two of us in the small private area I lean down and kiss her sweet lips. Then I whisper in her ear, "Vita, I love you, baby, and I'm here with you. You're not alone, my love."

Gazing down at my beautiful woman I feel completely helpless, but I know she just needs some time to get better. I pull a small metal chair up to her bed, reach for her hand, and hold it between mine.

A nurse comes in so I ask, "Do you know how long until she wakes and is alert?"

"Because of the complications she had with the anesthesia it may take several hours, or longer. We just aren't sure."

"Is this the last visiting hour until tomorrow?"

"Yes, ma'am it is. But please don't worry, we are taking extra care with her, Miss Kennedy."

"Thank you, Miss…..?

"It's Carter. I'm Margaret Carter, and I'm Vita's Nurse."

"I appreciate everything you are doing for Vita."

"Miss Kennedy. Someone mentioned your name and I couldn't believe you were here in our hospital. I have some of your books and read them often."

I smile at her and am elated that I have an ally in the hospital. I may need it. "Well, thank you, Margaret. I hope my books have been helpful."

"Oh yes they are indeed. It's very nice meeting you, and don't worry I'll take good care of your niece."

"That makes me happy, thank you so much, Margaret."

As she leaves, I continue holding Vita's hand, staying as long as they allow, maintaining the role of a concerned and loving aunt. I hate lying, but I can guarantee that I wouldn't even be allowed in the hospital if they knew the real nature of our relationship. Why does it have to be this way? Why can't I just tell them that we are a couple and in love? I shake my head, knowing that isn't even a remote possibility.

I look at my watch and see that I've been with Vita much longer than the time allowed for visits. I kiss her hand again as I continue gazing at my love. I stand and lean over her and whisper, "Baby, you have to continue to be strong, and get well." I kiss her sweet lips again and whisper, " I want to see your lovely curves in those khaki pants and sexy boots riding your motorcycle for me."

As I sit back down I notice the nurse, Margaret standing at her bedside. I gaze at her knowing she obviously heard every word I said to Vita, and the kiss. She looks at me and smiles then says, "Miss Kennedy, don't worry. We are the only two people in this hospital that know Vita isn't your niece."

I kiss Vita's hand as I continue looking at Margaret. "I

saw your love for her immediately. I have a lovely woman that I'm deeply in love with as well," she whispers.

I begin to cry, to sob. Finally, I'm allowed to release my internal grief. Margaret touches my shoulder and says. No one is back here but me and one other nurse, I'm going to let you stay for as long as you want. Or until one of the doctors kicks you out." She snickers.

"Thank you, Margaret. She's everything to me."

Margaret nods and then begins taking Vita's vitals as I continue gazing at my love.

Back in the waiting room I glance at my watch and see that it's almost 3:00 AM. Margaret allowed me to stay with Vita until almost midnight. I left shortly before the doctor checked in on her. I've drifted in and out of sleep, clutching Vita's Jacket that has kept me warm and safe for the last several hours.

As I cover my mouth and nose and inhale Vita's scent I see Hazel approaching me. Oh hell, I am sure she watched me inhaling Vita. I rise to greet her, "Hazel, I'm glad you're here."

"How is she, Kate?"

I inform Hazel about the complications from the anesthesia and mention that I was able to stay with her until midnight.

"She still wasn't awake when I left, and there hasn't been any updates since then."

Hazel nods her head then glances at Vita's jacket and meets my eyes. I quickly ask, "How was the train ride?"

"Long. Very long. I didn't think I'd ever get here."

"Well, I'm glad you're here, Hazel."

She stares at me for what seems like forever then asks, "Are you sure about that?"

"Of course, Hazel, why would you ask that?"

Hazel looks around the waiting area. No one is in here but the two of us so she begins. "Kate, I know something is different between you and Vita, don't you dare deny it."

I begin crying, then sobbing again. Damn! I'm so mad at myself, how could she possibly know?

I pull myself together then look at Hazel and say, "I won't ever deny it, Hazel. I love Vita with everything in me. You probably hate me right now, but I'll never, ever, deny my love for her."

Hazel sits back in her chair and I can tell she is stewing. I don't say another word as we both sit in silence for a while.

"Kate, right now part of me wants to have you escorted out of this hospital. How could you have let this happen? You're almost old enough to be her Mother for god's sake. I trusted you with her. I knew from the start it was a bad idea allowing Vita to be your driver."

I feel a sudden force of anger that pushes the tears away. "Hazel, you didn't allow anything. Vita is a twenty-eight year old woman who decided that for herself."

"Kate, I want you to leave."

"Hazel, I love her, and I'm not going anywhere."

"If you don't leave Vita alone I'll smear your name from one end of this country to the other. You are fully aware that I have the connections as your personal assistant to do that."

I look at her in disbelief and say, "Do you know what would come from that, Hazel?"

She shoots her head around at me and sharply asks, "What?"

"All you would be doing is smearing Vita's name as well, and hurting me financially which would also hurt Vita's financial security. If you take away my earning potential, it will affect Vita too, because we are committed to one another, and nothing is going to tear us apart."

"Damn you, Kate!"

"Hazel, you can't possibly believe that I'm the first woman that Vita has been with. Can you?"

Hazel sighs sharply and doesn't say anything for a few moments. Then she says, "Maybe I do know that. But Kate, it's been with women her own age. My god you've practically watched Vita grow up."

"Miss Kennedy?" Hazel and I both jump up and rush to the voice. It's a younger gentleman. A doctor.

"Yes, I'm Miss Kennedy, how is Vita?"

"She is beginning to wake up now. We were quite concerned for a while, but I believe she is going to be just fine. Thank goodness you got her here so quickly, if you hadn't her appendix would have ruptured. We will be moving her into a room within the next couple of hours. Someone will let you know when she is moved and you can visit her in her room then."

"Thank you doctor, Hazel says."

I begin to cry, almost uncontrollably as I walk back to my seat leaving Hazel standing. All I can think of is how much I want to hold Vita in my arms again knowing she is going to be okay.

Hazel walks back over and sits beside me again, but doesn't speak. After a moment she says, "Thank you for getting Vita here so quickly."

"That is something that I don't need a thank you for, Hazel. But I appreciate you saying it under the circumstances."

"Kate, I wasn't worried about you crossing the line with Vita; I was worried that she would. I am fully aware that Vita has looked up to you since her teenage years. And perhaps

I've known she has loved you since then. It's just hard to swallow."

I wait a minute before I speak. "I'm sure it is Hazel, but I intend on taking care of Vita for the rest of my life, or for as long as she wants me."

"This just complicates everything. How am I supposed to continue working with you now? It would be impossible."

"Oh Hazel, I don't know. It's all so new for you, and for us as well. But Hazel, I love you, and don't want you to leave because of this. You told me the Friday before we all went to dinner that I'm family. Do you remember?"

Hazel nods but doesn't look at me.

"Well, we really are family now, I suppose." We continue sitting in silence after that comment. I know Hazel is mad, disappointed in me and most likely wants to slap me, but hopefully when Vita wakes she will calm down.

Vita is in a room now and despite Hazel's threats she hasn't had me thrown out of the hospital, yet. I assume she knows she would be in deep trouble if Vita woke without me by her side.

We are sitting on opposite sides of Vita's bed while I continue to hold her hand and watch her. She begins to softly say, "Kate. Kate, sweetheart."

I squeeze her hand and say, "Vita, I'm here, love."

"I love you, Kate," she whispers.

"I love you, Vita. I'm still here and am not leaving you, baby."

Hazel remains quiet then leaves the room. I take the opportunity to kiss Vita's sweet lips. "Vita, baby, you're mine and I love you so much." I watch a sweet smile form and it completely melts my heart.

Hazel comes back in and stands by her bed, takes Vita's other hand and holds it. Vita whispers, "Grandma?"

"Yes, Vita. It's me dear."

Vita says, "Good. I love you too, Grandma."

I watch Hazel's eyes fill with tears then she says, "I love you, little Vita."

A nurse enters the room and begins checking Vita's vitals again which startles Vita awake. The nurse says, "Well, welcome back, Miss St. John."

I immediately stand to catch a glimpse of those velvety eyes of hers, the ones that have held me captive for days.

She smiles tenderly at me, "Hi sweetheart," she softly says.

"Hello, love." I say then wink at her which makes her giggle.

Vita turns and looks at Hazel and smiles. "I'm glad you're here Grandma."

"Well Vita, of course I'm here."

After the nurse leaves Vita starts to become more alert and even tries to rise up. "Vita, honey, you have to stay in bed." I sit on the edge of the bed and our eyes catch and she smiles at me again.

"Kate, please tell me the last several days haven't been a dream."

Kissing her hand with Hazel standing there I say, "No, Vita. You haven't been dreaming. I love you with all my heart, baby."

"Good," she says and then giggles. "What happened to me?"

I explain everything to Vita as she watches me with those sweet eyes of hers, never unlocking mine. "Well, I didn't mean to be so much trouble."

"Oh Vita, you could never be too much of anything."

Hazel laughs and says, "I disagree, Vita you are always too much!"

We all three laugh.

"I know Grandma. I take after you."

"I suppose you do, little Vita. So you can't help it."

Vita looks at me for a while and then at Hazel. I can see that brain of hers at work. Suddenly, her eyes pool with tears then she glances at Hazel, "Grandma, I love Kate. You know I always have, and I want to be with her, forever. She loves me, Grandma."

How did Vita know to say this now? Did she sense mine and Hazel's uneasiness with one another? I look at Hazel who is nodding with tearful eyes.

"Vita, I've always known you loved Kate. I didn't know how much though, until now. It's hard at the moment, but I suppose I'll get used to it. After all, I love Kate too, and I always have."

"Thank you, Hazel, and I love you."

CHAPTER ELEVEN: VITA

Kate and I sit side by side on the deck of our rented beach cottage in Atlantic City, as the late afternoon sun casts a warm glow around us. "Sweetheart, thank you for bringing me here to heal. You always know how to make me happy. This reminds me of Wilmington—the night I kissed you on the beach for the first time."

"Vita, I still remember how you walked away from the water toward me. I felt your eyes on me and I was completely frozen until you reached up, touched my cheek and your sweet lips met mine. They were soft and cool and your lips tasted of moonlight and sea salt. You were already mine, but after that kiss I knew I would never let you go."

"That's such a lovely memory, Kate, and that night was magical. Just like this moment, here with you, in the late afternoon."

"Vita, I can't think of a more appropriate place for you to heal before we return to Savannah. This is for me too. I intend on taking care of you, and spoiling you for the next several weeks as you heal."

"Kate, I've been thinking. Would you go into town and purchase an underwood typewriter for me and some paper?"

"Of course I will. Are you thinking of writing, love?"

"Yes I am. You know I've loved you since before I can remember and I've admired the way you write and encourage people. Not only have I fallen deeply in love with you, but you've inspired me to write as well."

Kate looks out at the water and doesn't speak for a moment. As a wave crashes, she looks at me with tears in her eyes and smiles. "Vita, I don't know what to say, love, other than I know you will be an amazing writer, baby."

"Thank you, sweetheart."

"Vita, I want to ask you something?"

"Sure, go ahead."

Kate turns toward me and looks seriously at me, "When they first admitted you to the hospital they gave me forms to fill out."

"Yes, I'm sure they did. What about them?"

Kate takes a deep breath then says, "It had a section for address and next of kin so I put my address in Savannah and my name."

"Well of course you did, I mean you were my Aunt then," I say and giggle.

Kate smiles but still looks seriously at me so I sit up slowly and turn toward her. "What's wrong, sweetheart?"

"When I wrote my address and my name I meant for that to be permanent. I was hell bent that you are mine so much that I didn't even want Hazel's name there."

"I am yours, Kate."

"Vita, I'm saying I want my home to be your permanent address. I want you to live with me, share my home as well as my life. It will be our home together. Will you live with me Vita?"

"Well, that depends, Kate."

"On what?"

"May I leave my motorcycle parked in your driveway?"

"Vita, you can park your motorcycle in my living room or anywhere you'd like if you'll agree to live with me for the rest of my life."

I look at her with a grin and say, "Let me think it over, sweetheart." As I try not to laugh.

Quickly I say, "I thought about it and yes, I'd love living with you, sweetheart. Kate I would have moved in with you ten years ago if you'd have asked me then."

Kate laughs loudly. "Wouldn't Hazel have loved that. Her eighteen year old granddaughter living with a thirty-four-year old woman. She would have killed me for sure. I'm lucky to be alive now."

I laugh as I hold my side again, "Kate, let me tell you something. I planned on moving in with you whether you asked me or not."

"Vita, you're a damn firecracker, I should have known."

"Seriously though Kate. Yes, I will share your home and life with you. You're all I've ever wanted since I can remember." I pull her hand to me and kiss it.

"Vita, you make me so happy."

"All I want, Kate, is to make you happy."

"My sweet, Vita. What did I do to deserve you?"

"Just by being your kind and wonderful self, Kate," I say to her.

We sit quietly for a while and enjoy the gentle coastal breeze. Having Kate beside me and this lovely ocean breeze is all the medicine I need to heal.

Kate speaks. "Vita, I love the idea of you writing, and I've been thinking."

"About what?"

"Theology School."

"Oh that again? Kate I need a break before I finish, plus I

am not going back to Atlanta and live without you. There's no way in hell that is happening. I've spent years aching for you, Kate, so I never want to know another day without you."

"Oh Vita, honey I'm not asking you to, love. And I feel the same. I want to see your beautiful face every morning when I wake, then kiss it sweetly every night before sleep."

I kiss Kate's hand and smile and then ask, "How would that work if I'm back in Atlanta?"

"Well, I was thinking of renting us a small home or apartment in Atlanta. I could write from there, do radio interviews and book signings. We could live together while you complete your degree. Weekends and holidays we could drive to Savannah to our home together."

I glance over at Kate. She is gazing at me intently.

"Well, sweetheart, I'll admit that I can live with that idea. But I don't want to go back until next fall. I have a book in my head that needs writing. I bet you have one as well."

Kate smiles at me and says, "Yes, I do as a matter of fact. It makes me incredibly happy, and proud that you want to write. We can start here, in Atlantic City. I'll buy two type-writers, and two tons of paper and we can write, laugh, and make love every single day for the next few weeks, or months."

"Sweetheart, that sounds amazing. I adore that idea," says Vita.

"So do I, love. We can be the sapphic version of Scott and Zelda Fitzgerald."

We both laugh. Then I ask, "Who gets to be Zelda?"

Kate laughs and says, "Well, Vita, you're so rebellious, free-spirited, and completely Southern, I suppose you get to be Zelda."

Holding my side as I laugh, "Well, you're my Southern lady too, however you have written many, many books like 'Scottie,' so I suppose you get to be him. However, in the bedroom, you are my sexy and seductress, Kate Kennedy."

"Vita, my love. I'll always be your seductress lover in the bedroom."

Kate smiles at me and leans towards me for a kiss. I pull her close and give her a deep passionate kiss as I grip her blonde locks of hair.

Kate pulls away and says, "Damn, Vita. My god woman you know how to drive me wild. No woman has ever done to me what you do." She shakes her head and sits back in her chair.

"Too bad we can't have sex," I say.

"Well, perhaps after a couple of weeks or so we can ease into it a bit. Nothing radical though, like 4:00 AM."

"Oh, Kate. stop! You're going to make me split my stitches open," I say as I laugh.

We look at one another and chuckle.

Kate gives me a sensual gaze and says, "Well, just because you can't have sex doesn't mean I can't." Then giggles.

"Kate Kennedy! What does that mean?!"

"Think about it for a moment, love. You're a clever girl you can figure it out," she says as she leans back, closes her eyes, and grins.

Kate jumps as I smack her with a newspaper then begins to laugh uncontrollably. "You want me to narrate 4:00 AM for you, don't you? And what will you be doing as I audibly replay it for you?"

Kate grins at me and says, "I think you know what I'll be doing, love."

"You're so naughty, I can't believe you. And what am I supposed to do after you've had your amazing orgasm leaving me full of lust?"

"Oh, Vita, you're such a delight, love. I'm just playing with you."

"No you aren't. I've come to realize what an animal you are in the bedroom." I sit quietly for a moment watching the waves tumble onto the beach. Then I glance back at Kate. She gives me a cute wink, and I melt. "Heaven's woman, you're too much," I say, holding my side as I laugh.

"I love you Vita. So very much."

"And I love you, sweetheart. Do you remember what I said that night at dinner when I found out you needed a driver?" Kate looks at me curiously; I see her mind working.

"I believe you said, 'I'll do it.'"

"It would actually give me quite a thrill watching you make yourself orgasm as I whisper naughty scenes in your ear."

"Vita! You're driving me crazy."

I stand up, reach for her hand and say, "Close those doors and lock them, then meet me in the bedroom, sweetheart. 4:00 AM awaits."

EPILOGUE: KATE

Six Weeks Later
December 1945
Atlantic City

I awaken to another glorious day at the beach, greeted by the early morning light. I turn to reach for Vita, but she's gone. As I rise and listen, all I hear is the faint sound of the waves breaking onto the shore.

I tie the sash of my robe as I walk through the cottage we rented weeks ago for Vita to heal from her Appendectomy.

"Vita. Where are you, love?" I ask. Then I see a typed note on the kitchen table.

Good Morning Sweetheart,
I'll be back soon, there is something that I need to do in town.
I took a Taxi, because I didn't need the Packard.
I'll explain when I get back. I have a surprise for you.

I think it will make you smile.
All my love…….Vita

As I pour myself a cup of coffee, I grin, and wait anxiously for Vita's return. I am so happy of her healing progress. She has made a remarkable and swift recovery. We could have left for Savannah two weeks ago. However, staying here with Vita, writing, and making love everyday has become completely addictive.

As I sip on my coffee I suddenly hear a familiar sound. I hear the enchanting deep throaty rumble of a motorcycle reverberating through the air and eventually stops in front of the cottage.

Opening the front door with my robe on and coffee in hand I see my young beautiful Vita atop a motorcycle similar to the one she rode up on that day she stole my heart.

Leaning against the frame of the door I give her a big smile as I see her wearing those sexy khaki pants that still fit her lovely body perfectly. Vita is smiling at me as our eyes lock and my heart begins to race again just as before.

Vita turns the motorcycle off, dismounts, and then struts up the sidewalk with that same sexy swagger as before, shaking those lovely curls. I glance and see her khakis are tucked into the black Jodhpur boots. She is smiling at me as she walks confidently towards me. I am totally captivated, just as I was before. But now I know this young woman is mine.

"Good morning, sweetheart," She says softly, as she pushes her fingers through those dark curls of hers.

I grin and blush a bit. I'd almost forgotten how damn tough and sexy she is like this.

"Well, good morning to you, love. Where did you get the motorcycle?" I ask as I keep grinning at her.

Vita leans in and kisses my lips tenderly. Then pushes the

door open and walks past me. I turn toward her. She takes my coffee cup and sits it on the side table. Then she grabs me around my hips, picks me up and spins me around the room and shouts, "Let's go for a ride, gorgeous."

"Vita, put me down, you silly woman."

"Only if you promise you'll ride with me."

I look down at her and see her love for me as I grab her sexy locks of dark curls. "I guess I have little choice."

Vita lets me down gently. Her intense gaze at me is almost too much. "How in the hell are you only twenty-eight years old, Vita St. John?"

She smiles at me and says, "Go change into something warm, sweetheart. We are riding the coast this morning."

"Oh, Vita. That sounds amazing. Give me a few minutes, love," I say before I dash to the bedroom to dress.

Walking back into the living room I see Vita smiling at me. "I assume you remember how I said I wanted to see you again in these khaki's, hugging your curves." Vita nods and asks, "Remember when I told you I packed them along with my boots?"

I nod and say, "Of course I do."

"Well, this is why, Kate. I knew by the end of our trip that you'd be mine. And I wanted to know how your arms would feel wrapped around me as the wind blew in my face and the love I have for you fills my heart."

"Vita, my love, you are such a beautiful soul. Come on then, let's both find out how that feels, baby."

I watch Vita quickly push down fast and firmly on the kickstart lever with her foot, just as she did the day I watched her from the sidewalk in front of my home. Then I hear the same deep throaty rumble and I smile. Vita climbs on top of this beast and says, "Come on, gorgeous. This seat is longer than mine, we have plenty of room."

"Aren't you going to give me a Kierkegaard quote first?" I ask loudly.

Vita laughs, closes her eyes briefly, opens them and shouts, "Life is not a problem to be solved, but a reality to be experienced!"

"That's beautiful, Vita!" I say then kiss her cheek.

I climb on the motorcycle and wrap my arms around her lovely waist and pull her close to me. She then turns toward me and asks, "Are you ready, Miss Kennedy?"

I lean in and smell Vita's soft curls and say, "Yes, love. Take me wherever you wish."

Vita laughs as we begin to glide in the wind. "I love you, Vita St. John!" I say loudly as I laugh with sweet freedom. As we ride along Route 9 I realize how much loving Vita has changed me.

Holding on tightly against Vita I gaze at the morning light reflecting on the Atlantic Ocean. It looks as though a million sparklers are exploding as the sun reflects its light against the water. The coastal views are breathtaking, but even more so with my arms wrapped around my brave and lovely, Vita. The woman I've loved since her youth.

EPILOGUE TWO: VITA

Nine Months Later
September 1946
Atlanta Georgia

K ate found us a perfect cottage to live in for the next year while I finish my Master's Program in Theology at Emory. We settled in about two weeks ago and my classes start next week. Originally, I hadn't planned on returning, but Kate's love and encouragement helped me to remember why I began this journey in the first place.

As I finish placing my books on the book cases I hear Kate enter the room. "Well, hello, my sexy school girl."

Turning towards her I laugh. "Kate, that actually made me wet. Damn woman, I suddenly felt like that teenager who fell in love with you years ago."

"Oh Vita. Well, we will always let that be our secret," She says and winks at me.

I look at the books in my hands and throw them up in the air and say, "Fuck this." Then I run and grab Kate who is screaming with laughter. "This is your fault, sweetheart." I take her hand and guide her to the bedroom and shut the door.

"Now I expect you to give your 'school girl' the orgasm of her life."

"You do? Hmmm, well I don't know, love. Don't you think I'm a bit too old for you?"

"Well, I don't know ma'am, why don't you check and see?" I ask as I unzip my slacks and remove them. Kate pulls me close, her gray eyes on mine. She reaches inside my panties then I feel her fingers touching me. I gasp and close my eyes. Her touch makes me weak. I know it always will.

"Well, my sweet Vita, you feel as though you're the perfect age for me. I mean you're soaked, love." She grabs some of my fluids and moves to my clit and gently touches it as I open my eyes to meet her love for me. The woman I've loved forever is holding my eyes captive as she seductively brings me close to orgasm.

I whisper, "Kate."

She smiles at me knowing what I feel for her. "Come for me, Vita." She whispers in my ear and she continues her soft circles on my clit. I've never orgasmed standing up, but I'm finding this moment quite erotic and intoxicating.

Kate whispers in my ear again, "I said, come for me, my sweet Vita." Oh damn, that did it. I begin to shake and grow weak. I wrap my arms around Kate's neck as she grabs me with incredible strength, holds my dark eyes captive and then watches me lose myself to her.

"Kate….Kate," I whisper as I have the sweetest orgasm of my life. It brings tears to my eyes and I can't help but almost fall on the floor. Kate pulls me to the bed then climbs on top of me.

"Vita, It's okay, baby," She sweetly says. I begin crying into her arms. Kate puts her arms around me and pulls me to her, holding me tight. She lets me continue crying in her arms. She has to know how sweet that intense moment was.

Kate gently pulls away to look into my eyes. She smiles at me and I realize just how safe I am in this woman's arms. "I love you, Kate."

She slips off of me onto her side. I turn towards her and smile a bit bashfully. She whispers, "It's okay, Vita. You're safe with me, baby." I nod and smile at her. We both lie together in silent peace. I touch her lips and trace the outline of them with my finger.

After a moment I rise up and prop my head on my hand. "Kate, something about that orgasm was different."

"What was different, Vita?" She whispers.

"I'm scared to tell you, Kate."

"Baby, you can tell me anything."

Immediately I wish I'd kept my mouth shut. But I didn't, so now I have to confess what happened to me. Kate is waiting patiently. Just as she always does, I love this about her. She never pushes for my thoughts, she always allows them to flow freely before I speak.

"Well, sweetheart. You know I am twenty-nine now, almost thirty. But, Kate, sweetheart,." I pause for a moment. "That was the eighteen-year old Vita who just orgasmed for you."

Kate reaches for me and looks into my eyes with love and whispers, "I know, Vita. I knew the whole time, love."

"You did, Kate? How?"

Kate's eyes pool with tears as she sits up on the side of the bed. I sit up next to her and place my arms around her, trying to be as patient as she always is.

I whisper, "How did you know that, Kate?"

Kate turns towards me and pushes my hair back with her fingers then she gazes into my eyes and says, "Because, that was the thirty-four year old Kate who was loving you."

We both look at one another completely stunned. "How did that happen, Kate? We've been together for almost eleven months."

"I don't know, Vita. Perhaps, it had to happen at some point so the younger version of our love could be set free. I don't believe it will happen again. You and I are two grown women in love with a healthy sex life. Let's not think too much about it, other than how special it was."

"So the young Vita was allowed to experience how Kate felt making love to her?"

Kate touches my cheek and nods, "Yes, Vita. I think that's exactly what happened."

I pull Kate to me and hug her tightly as I smile. Then I whisper, "Please tell her: It was beautiful."

THANK YOU

Thanks for reading Driving Miss Kennedy. I hope you enjoyed it.

I'd love it if you could take a minute to leave a review on Amazon and let me know what You thought.

Thanks,
Aven Blair

ALSO BY AVEN BLAIR

Claire's Young Flame

Evan's Entanglement

Julian's Lady Luck

My Sapphires Only Dance for Her

Sailing Mrs. Clarkson

ABOUT THE AUTHOR

 Aven is a passionate Sapphic romance author living in a charming Southern U.S. town with her wife and their two mischievous Chihuahuas. She crafts compelling narratives about strong Southern women navigating love and life, often set in historical Southern America. Her stories feature steamy age-gap romances, rich with warmth, humor, and depth, captivating readers with unforgettable tales of unwavering dedication.

Printed in Great Britain
by Amazon